"I guess it's just you and me for dinner," Tom said.

Jenna realized how it must look to him. "Oh, I wasn't inviting myself over."

"Having dinner with you is certainly more appealing than what I had planned for tonight."

"Which was what?" she asked. "I don't want to keep you from your plans."

"That's just it. I didn't have any."

"You don't have much company?"

"I just moved here—I don't know anyone."

"You know me."

Tom smiled. "I'm getting there."

Her insides hummed in a way she hadn't felt for quite some time. His startling blue eyes locked on to hers and she actually felt her hands begin to sweat.

"I don't want the food to

He didn't look away wh
from the table and waite

A gentleman. Or a gentle
was flattering to have a man treat her like a lady again after all this time.

D1065040

Books by Lisa Mondello

Love Inspired

Fresh-Start Family

Love Inspired Suspense

Cradle of Secrets
Her Only Protector
Yuletide Protector

LISA MONDELLO

Lisa's love of writing romance started early when she penned her first romance novel (a full fifty-eight pages long, but who's counting) at the age of ten. She then went on to write a mystery script that impressed her sixth-grade teacher so much he let her and her friends present it as a play to the whole grade. There was no stopping her after that! After studying sound recording technology in college and managing a Boston rock band for four years, she settled down with her husband of more than eighteen years and raised a family. Although she's held many jobs through the years, ranging from working with musicians and selling kitchen and catering tools, to teaching first- and second-graders with special needs how to read and write, her love of writing has always stayed in the forefront, and she is now a full-time freelance writer. In many ways writing for Steeple Hill Books feels like coming home. Lisa lives in Western Massachusetts with her husband, four children (who never cease to amaze her as they grow), a very pampered beagle and a rag doll cat who thinks she owns them all.

Fresh-Start Family
Lisa Mondello

Steeple
Hill®

Published by Steeple Hill Books™

STEEPLE HILL BOOKS

Steeple
Hill®

ISBN-13: 978-0-373-81508-1

FRESH-START FAMILY

Though he fall, he shall not be utterly cast down:
for the Lord upholds him with his hand.
—*Psalms* 37:24

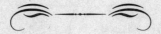

This book is dedicated to the men and women who serve in all branches of the United States Military.

Chapter One

"**P**lease open up! It's a matter of life and death!" Jenna Atkins, panting from her run through the rain, listened for movement inside the farmhouse. She prayed that the little slice of light she'd seen when she'd driven by at this late hour meant that her new neighbors had moved in and that they were awake.

With the heel of her wet palm, she banged on the door again and waited, peeking through the sheer curtain for signs of movement. Cupping her hands against the windowpane, she strained to see. There was still a light on inside. Someone *had* to be awake.

Finally, the thud of feet hitting the floor let Jenna know she'd been heard. Her lips quivered and her body trembled from the cold seeping into her bones. She had only a moment to notice the curtain in the porch window lifting and then falling back into place before the person suddenly disappeared from view.

Within seconds the porch light blazed and the door swung open wide. Shielding her eyes from the sudden blast of light, she found a man standing at the threshold, taking up every inch of space in the doorway with intimidating height that was only slightly less menacing than his eyes. She couldn't make out their color, but the dark outline that puffed beneath them was telling, letting her know she'd interrupted his sleep. His dusty blue sweatshirt was slightly hiked up on one side. He probably wasn't even fully awake.

Guilt invaded her, but she instantly pushed it aside. Her baby needed her.

"Please, help me. It's an emergency!"

Tag opened his eyes as wide as he could to focus on the person standing on his porch. The yellow blur resolved into a rain-slicker-covered woman. She looked like a wet mop, Tag thought as he peered down at her, trying not to scowl. But he knew it was there. Abject fatigue didn't exactly bring out his charm.

Life and death. Had he been dreaming that part?

"I need your help. It's an emergency," she repeated.

He blinked the rest of the sleep out of his eyes as best he could and took a better look at her. The woman's eyes were red rimmed, as if she'd been crying, her obvious distress distracting him from the slightly upturned nose, the bow-shaped lips and those blue eyes the color of gems.

"What seems to be the problem?" he asked, raking his fingers over his head.

"My son needs to get to the hospital in Valentine. We were on our way, but my truck broke down just up the road from your house."

He glanced out into the darkness. "You walked all the way here in the rain?"

"No. I ran."

"Why do you need to go to Valentine? It's nearly a two-hour drive from here. If it's an emergency and your son is hurt, why not go to the clinic right here in Chesterfield?"

She shook her head impatiently. "They aren't equipped to handle Brian's needs. They'll only stabilize him and then send him by ambulance to one of the other major hospitals in the state. He needs to get to a major medical facility now."

"You can use the phone to call someone for a ride, if you need to."

"The sheriff runs an ambulance service, I was hoping I could use your phone to call him, and I can have the ambulance bring us to Valentine. Once I call the emergency number to let Sheriff Wayne know where we are, he'll meet us and drive us to Valentine himself."

"Where is your son now?" Tag asked, giving a quick look behind her into the darkness before stepping away from the door and motioning the woman to come in.

"I need to use your phone," she said, ignoring his question.

"Yes, of course."

Tag closed the door as the woman stepped into his living room, and took a second to peer past the curtain to see if he'd missed anyone else outside on the porch. When he turned around, the woman was frantically searching his living room.

"Your son?"

"Your phone?" They both spoke at the same time.

He pointed to the far end of the living room. "The phone is in the kitchen. Right down the hall. You didn't leave your son out in the rain, did you?"

He followed her as she made her way to the kitchen.

"Of course not! Well, yes, in a way. He's in the car with my father."

Tag nodded, watching the woman as she first snatched the phone out of the cradle, and then stood there with a lost expression. With the phone gripped tightly in her hand, she closed her eyes, her hands visibly trembling. Frustration filled her expression, but Tag could see her struggle to contain her emotions and stay calm.

"The storm seems to have knocked out your phone line," she said at last. And though her voice was quiet, Tag could hear the panic behind it.

He knew the sound of that fear, how it could take hold of you, suffocating the life out of a person. He'd felt it enough times himself over the years to understand how crippling it could be.

Something took him over in that moment, an instinct honed from years of rigorous military training that led him to take charge of difficult situations when faced with the seemingly impossible. Whatever it was, it wrapped around Tag and had him gripping the woman by the upper arms.

His voice was calm and even as he spoke. He

looked directly into her face. "Look at me. Your son needs to get to the hospital immediately, right?"

"Yes," she answered.

"Then there is no time to waste finding a working phone and waiting for the ambulance. But you have to listen to me and do what I tell you to, okay?"

As he turned away, he heard her soft prayer of thanks. His heart squeezed. He didn't want to acknowledge why right now. He knew he could help her. He had it within his means to do that much, and not even two years out of military life had taken away the drive from him to save the day, inasmuch as he could.

He let go of the woman's arms and grabbed his jacket from the coat hook in the mudroom. Then pulled on his boots.

"Listen to me…I'm sorry. What's your name?" he asked.

"Jenna."

"Jenna," he repeated. "The keys to my truck are on the counter. Take them, pick up your son and your father and bring them back here."

Jenna shook her head, her face perplexed. "But we need to get to the hospital."

"Yes. That's why I want you to drive around to

the back of the yard and follow the road that cuts through the field. Once you're there, you'll see a small prop plane."

Her eyes widened. "You have a plane?"

"Yes, a small Cessna, but it's big enough to carry the three of you. I'll fly you to Valentine. We'll make much better time in the air than trying to navigate these back roads. We can radio ahead to the hospital and have an ambulance meet us at the airport."

She let out a sigh of relief, her face draining of the worry that had plagued it just moments earlier. She quickly scouted the counter until she found his keys. "Can you fly in this weather?"

A slight smile tugged at Tag's cheeks. He'd flown in all kinds of weather and conditions in the ten years he'd been a marine. A little drizzle wasn't enough to ground him. Besides, while they'd been talking, the storm had started to slow down. Flying would be easier now that the torrential rain had died back to a light drizzle. He only hoped the rain hadn't washed out the makeshift airstrip he planned to use to get the plane off the ground.

"It isn't a problem. I'm more concerned with whether or not you know how to drive a stick shift."

"Yeah. My father's truck has a manual transmission."

"Good, then you shouldn't have any problem. Get going and I'll meet you out back."

Tag watched silently as she flew out the door, leaving it ajar.

Jenna was out of his sight before he'd had time to move. The sound of his old faithful pickup firing to a roar was followed by the spray of gravel and dirt from spinning tires. Within moments the bright taillights of his truck bobbed down his driveway.

Tag's pulse urgently pounded against his eardrums. A rush of adrenaline—something he hadn't felt in a long time—kicked him into high gear. It wasn't just because he'd been woken out of a sound sleep. It was that sense of urgency, that rush of life, that made him feel alive. He'd loved this feeling back when he'd been in the service— the thrill of knowing that his actions and his skill had the power to make a difference in someone's life.

Jenna. That was what she'd said her name was. And she had a sick child who needed emergency medical treatment.

Tag pushed past memories that flooded his mind and had him catching his breath. Tender memories that still haunted him, keeping him awake at night. He focused instead on the task at hand as he strode through the drizzling darkness toward the narrow path between the crop fields.

While he waited for Jenna and her son, Tag quickly did a thorough check through of the twin-engine Cessna. He also took a quick walk with the flashlight to make sure the earlier rainfall hadn't created any potholes in the ground he was using for takeoff.

He gave each step its due. That was the only way to prevent missing a problem that could spell trouble during flight. But preparation for flying and getting behind the controls of a plane had almost become as natural as breathing to him after all these years.

He'd been drawn to the skies as a child, and it had been the very reason he'd chosen to enlist in the military after finishing college.

And now, all these years later, flying still gave him solace. When Tag was up in the air, he didn't feel the PTS—post-traumatic stress—that had ended his military career. And with a combination of lots of flying and a complete separation from military life, the PTS appeared to be fading. Instead of nightmares every night, now he seemed to have only flashbacks when something triggered a memory. The flashbacks had become less frequent these last few months. So much so that Tag had all but forgotten them, especially when he was flying.

He couldn't help but wonder what kinds of memories having a child on his plane might trigger. But he didn't have time to worry about that. Minutes counted when dealing with a sick or injured person, and Tag had trained hard to think quickly and act in emergencies.

The engine of the plane hummed as it warmed. He was just about finished with his flight check when Tag caught the headlights of his truck cutting a path toward his driveway, toward his narrow airstrip.

When the truck tires ground to a halt, he saw that Jenna was no longer sitting behind the wheel. Instead, she was sitting in the passenger's seat, cradling a small child in her lap. She waited until the older gentleman—she'd said her father had been with the boy—bolted from the driver's side and ran over to open her door. The older man lifted the young boy in his arms and loosely draped the blanket around him.

Jenna didn't bother to put the hood of her rain

slicker back on her head as she ran from the truck to the plane.

"This is my father, Ben," she called out as she ran.

"Good to meet you." Tag nodded a greeting to Ben.

"Likewise. Are you ready to take off?" Ben asked.

"Just about," said Tag.

They were shielded from the rain as they stood beneath the wing by the door. "If we're going to get up into the air, we need to climb aboard," Tag said.

"I'll be driving," Ben said.

"There's room for four people," Tag replied.

"We'll need the truck to get back," said Ben.

Tag didn't bother to argue, just gripped the handhold as he climbed into the plane and readied a spot for the boy. He placed a small blanket over the seat and turned toward the door.

"Okay. I'm ready for him," he said, reaching his arms out to Ben.

Ben turned to Jenna. "Okay, then, I'll meet you there. You go with Brian. I'll be there as soon as I can get that heap started again—"

"Heap?" Tag interrupted. "You don't have time to bother with your vehicle now. Take my truck.

You'll have plenty of time to fix whatever is wrong with your truck later."

Ben's eyes widened at Tag's offer. "You'd do that? You don't even know us."

"We need to get the boy to the hospital. We can't waste any more time."

"Thank you," Ben said, carefully handing over the young boy with a relieved sigh.

Tag tried not to look at the child's face, knew already it might be his undoing. He'd always had a soft spot for kids, especially those in need. As gently as if he was holding a tiny bubble that would burst in his hands, he eased the boy over to his seat.

"I've never been in a plane before."

The voice that drifted to Tag's ears was small, soft and weak. Tag glanced down at the small bundle he'd held as he carefully secured the safety belt. The blanket mostly hid Brian, but from what he could see, the boy's eyes were dark and round. A brush of Tag's knuckles against Brian's cheek told him the child indeed had a whopper of a fever. Tag wondered if the doelike expression was from the fever or fear.

He swallowed the hard lump that was lodged in his throat and looked away. "Don't you worry, Scout," he said, hoping to reassure the child. "I've done this a time or two before." He swallowed again, this time in an effort to get that familiar lump down to a manageable spot. Poor kid. He was probably as terrified as his mother. "Your name is Brian, son?"

"Yes," Jenna answered, climbing into the plane.

"Nice to meet you, Brian. You just keep close to your mama and we'll be there soon."

Tag turned away and peered out the open hatch. Ben stood by the truck, staring at them, a look of desperation on his face. He would probably watch until the nose of the plane lifted into the air. He'd then jump in the truck and push the pedal to the floor the whole way to the hospital. With any luck, none of the roads between here and Valentine would be washed out and Ben would make good time.

The sooner he got there, the better because Jenna was going to need someone at the other end of this trip. And right now all she had was him.

As Tag buckled himself in and taxied down the makeshift airstrip between his fields, he recalled Jenna's soft prayer of thanks to God in the kitchen when he'd told her he would help her. A Christian woman, no doubt. That was good—it would comfort her to know the Lord was by her side in times like this. Jenna shouldn't have to be alone.

And Lord knew he was no kind of man to lean on.

Chapter Two

As the nose of the small plane inched its way into the black sky, Jenna's stomach did an acrobatic roll. Then another. She gathered Brian closer to her and squeezed her eyes shut.

Please, Lord, let us get to the hospital quickly.

Jenna didn't have the same phobia of flying her father did. Well, not quite as severe, anyway. But she'd never gotten past her apprehension for takeoffs and landings, even though, unlike Brian, this trip was far from the first time Jenna had flown in a plane. Thanks to her late husband, she had plenty of experience in the air. But she didn't want any of those memories to come charging back now, when she needed to focus on her son.

She held on to Brian in the backseat and trembled, the cold from her run in the rain finally seeping into her bones, praying his fever had stabilized.

"Are you doing okay, honey?" she asked Brian.

He nodded, wide-eyed and quiet. She hated that this was Brian's first time in a small plane. When he was feeling well, he was an adventure seeker who'd love flying in a plane like this, and would probably have asked Tag fifty questions already. It broke her heart that he couldn't even enjoy this opportunity, thanks to the fever. She didn't dare hope there'd be other chances. If her late husband had lived, Brian most likely would have already logged plenty of flight time with his dad given the fact that Kent had been a veteran air force pilot. But Kent wasn't there for them anymore. And truthfully, he hadn't made much of an effort even when he'd been alive.

Kent hadn't been inclined to be much of a father at all, especially to a child who wasn't healthy, and Jenna had made peace with that long ago. Soon after Brian's birth, they'd discovered the gravity of their son's fragile condition when he was diagnosed with polycystic kidney syndrome. Her marriage to a man she'd once loved enough to follow around the world had soon crumbled under the weight of Brian's medical troubles. Learning to do without Kent's support was a trick she'd mastered long before his death.

Right now she just needed to get through the next few hours, until she heard in the doctor's own words that Brian would be all right, that this sudden temperature wasn't the start of the collapse of Brian's remaining kidney. She could be strong for Brian until then.

"How long do you think the flight will take?" she asked. In all the confusion she realized she'd never learned her neighbor's name.

"Not long. The wind is on our side, so it should take about forty minutes or so."

"Wow. That fast, huh?"

"We don't follow highways in the sky. We've got a nice straight line ahead of us," he said. "And things should move pretty fast when we land, too. When I radioed my flight plan in, I asked the tower to contact the hospital so they could expect Brian. There'll be an ambulance waiting for us right on the tarmac."

Jenna nodded and looked out the window into the darkness, a mixture of relief and anxiety coursing through her.

"The real estate broker who sold me the house made it a point to mention Chesterfield had a hospital," he said next. "I thought it was equipped for emergencies."

"It is for most emergencies. Simple bone break or a bad flu. But my son was born with kidney disease. If his fever has anything to do with his kidneys, they can't handle it there. He was born with only one kidney, and it's not working properly. Whenever he spikes a temperature, like tonight, it could be…bad."

The plane hit an air pocket and bobbed, then shook. Her stomach lurched, and she focused on her son to take her mind off it.

Any other time her son's curious nature would have had him unable to contain himself in his seat. Instead, he was slumped back against her, virtually still.

"I'm sorry. I just realized I never even asked your name," she finally said, slightly embarrassed.

The man turned back briefly and said, "Tag."

"Tag? That's an unusual name. Is it short for something else?"

From the angle at which she was sitting, she watched the corner of his mouth lift into a quick smile. "It's what people called me in the marines. I've gotten so used to it, I rarely introduce myself by my real name." He turned quickly to her and said, "Tom. Tom Garrison."

"It's nice to meet you, Tom," she said. "I wish it were under less stressful circumstances, though."

Tom nodded a reply and kept his eyes on the controls of the plane as it bobbed and pitched in the weather.

She heaved a sigh, hoping to find the words for the small talk she'd need to stay calm. Her father knew how to chatter nonstop to keep her mind distracted on the long drive. But her father wasn't here. So if she wanted conversation to take her mind off just how quiet and still Brian was, it would be up to her.

Jenna needed to talk about nonsense. Surely Tag could concentrate on flying and talk about some senseless topic at the same time.

"How does your wife like the new farm?" she finally asked.

Tom's hand stiffened on the controls as soon as the words left her mouth, and she groaned silently. Had she brought up a touchy subject? She hadn't recalled seeing anyone downstairs with him. She hadn't been in a clear frame of mind when she'd stormed his door earlier, but she didn't remember any sign someone else was even in the house. Was he going through a divorce? Was that why he'd moved to her small town—to get away from it all?

After a long hesitation, Tom answered, "I live alone."

"Oh, I see."

Embarrassed, she looked away and glanced down at Brian. He appeared to be snoozing against her—another bad sign, if not even the excitement of being on a plane was enough to keep him awake.

Bending her head, she kissed his scorching forehead and continued her small talk.

"Your farm has been vacant for almost two years. I was surprised, and thrilled, to see the lights on when we drove by. Have you been here long?"

"Little over a week."

"That might explain why I haven't seen you around town."

He shrugged. "I'm not likely to be found around town much. I spend most of my day working the fields. They're quite a mess now. And there is still a lot of repair work needed to the barn and fences. If I'm not working the farm, I'm usually in the air."

In the air, she thought, remembering how Kent had filled all his free time in much the same way. Of course, with him, it had been an attempt to avoid home life. She forced her thoughts away from the bone of contention that had plagued her marriage. On nights like this, old resentments had a way of resurfacing.

Reaching for something to say, she added, "It's good that you're giving the farm some care, then. My father said that Mr. Nelson was old and sick for quite a while before his son finally convinced him to sell the property and move out to Michigan with him. I'm sure he's glad that someone is taking care of things for him here, even if the farm doesn't belong to him anymore. I never knew Mr. Nelson had an airstrip on his property, though."

Tom smiled. "It's not an airstrip, really. It is just an access road running through the fields. But it's level and straight and works like a charm as an airstrip. First thing I did when I moved in was modify the road with lights so I could fly."

Jenna thought back to their takeoff. She hadn't really been paying too much attention at the time. She had been more concerned with making sure Brian was securely strapped in and comfortable, but they certainly hadn't appeared to have any problems. Whatever modifications Tom had made had definitely paid off.

She smiled. "Brian told me at breakfast the other day that a plane had flown overhead and woken him up. I told him it was too soon in the season for someone to be out dusting crops. Some of the farmers around here have planes they use for dusting crops. Those are usually the only planes we see around here. Was that you? If so, I owe my son an apology."

"Guilty. I like seeing the sun kiss the horizon in the morning. Sorry I woke your son."

Jenna chuckled. "Mr. Garrison, I'm not sorry at all. You have a plane, and right now that makes you my new best friend."

"It's Tom. And I'm happy to help." He turned briefly and glanced at Brian. "How's he doing?"

Jenna stroked her son's cheek. "Still really feverish."

"Has he been like this long?"

"It always comes on quick with him. Brian will be playing, and before I know it, he's limp and tired. Tonight he went to bed fine and then just woke up drenched from the fever."

She didn't like the sudden shift in conversation to Brian's health. She wanted their talk to be a distraction from her fears.

"Did you learn to fly in the marines?" she asked, knowing in advance Tag probably had. Kent had learned to fly in the military. Sometimes she wondered what their life together would have been like if he hadn't joined the service. If he'd been on the ground instead of in the air when his kidneys had failed. Would they have been able to save him?

She quickly dismissed the thought. She couldn't change what had happened to Kent. The military hadn't been what killed him, or what destroyed their marriage. It was merely a means for Kent to escape from the one thing that had pushed a wedge between them, their son's illness.

"Actually," Tom said, "I learned to fly before I joined. Flying missions in the marines just gave me the means to do what I love. You still buckled?"

His quick change of subject threw Jenna off balance. She had to glance down at her lap and touch her buckle to make sure. "Yes. Is there a problem?"

Her heart picked up an extra beat.

"We're coming in to Valentine. We'll be landing shortly."

"Already?"

"The wonders of modern flight. I'll check with the tower to make sure our ambulance has arrived."

She gently nudged Brian to wake him. He was sick and probably wouldn't care one way or the other, but it was his first airplane landing, and she didn't want him to miss it. As she looked out the window, she could see the runway lights. It was an awesome view. Under normal circumstances it was something she was sure her son would enjoy.

"Brian, we're getting ready to land. Do you want to look at the lights, honey?" she said softly with her lips against his forehead.

His skin was still scorching to the touch. The lip test, she'd always called it. When he was much younger, he used to refuse to let her take his temperature. Instead, she'd lavish him with kisses. She'd gotten so good that she could gauge the severity of his fever based on just that. He was older now and didn't fight with her about using the thermometer anymore. Still, tonight she didn't even have to take his temperature to know they needed to go to the emergency room pronto.

As they landed at the airport and taxied down the runway, she saw the flashing lights of the ambulance waiting for them. A mixture of apprehension and relief washed over her.

When the plane came to a stop, the EMTs moved the gurney into place as Tom opened the door. A rush of cold air hit Jenna's face as a whirlwind of activity centered on Brian. Her heart raced watching them place her son on the gurney and strap him in.

"This way, ma'am," one of the EMTs said as they moved toward the ambulance. After they loaded Brian, Jenna lifted one foot up to climb into the back, but stopped and turned.

Tom was standing by the plane, shutting the cockpit door.

"Aren't you coming to the hospital?" she called out.

His eyes widened. "Ah, um. I need to secure the plane."

"Oh, right."

"Ma'am?" The EMT motioned for her to climb in.

"Yes, coming." She blinked as the bright lights inside the ambulance stung her eyes.

She looked back toward the plane one more time as she sat down next to the gurney.

Tom waved and called out, "I'll meet you at the hospital when I'm done."

She nodded and they shut the door.

As the ambulance sped toward the road and the EMTs took Brian's vital signs, she held Brian's hand and wondered what on earth she'd been thinking, assuming Tom would be coming with them. She'd just met the man. He'd done a wonderful thing helping her tonight by flying her and Brian to Valentine. There was no reason for him to come to the hospital.

The look of surprise on his face should have clued her in that her assumption he'd join them was wrong. He probably wanted nothing more than to get back in his plane and fly home. Now she'd guilted him into babysitting her until her father arrived.

The ride to the hospital was a little surreal. Jenna answered questions when she was asked, and kept quiet as the EMTs worked with Brian. She'd been through this before. It didn't make it any easier.

When they reached the hospital, Brian was taken in to the E.R. As soon as the doctor ordered an ultrasound of Brian's kidney, she took that moment to slip out and collect herself in the waiting room. She was both surprised and elated to find Tom there.

His face registered alarm at the sight of her.

"What's wrong? Why aren't you in with Brian?"

Jenna tried to smile. "Dr. Healy was already here when we arrived. He took Brian down right away to do an ultrasound of his kidney to see if there are any new cysts or changes."

His brow furrowed with a puzzled expression. "Why didn't you go with them?"

She heaved a sigh and tried her best to stand tall. "I've learned that when Brian is in a crisis like this, I need a moment to collect myself once I get him to the hospital. If I don't, I'll break down in front of Brian, and I can't do that. I need only a minute or two. With the ultrasound as a distraction, I know Brian will be okay without me until I get back in there." The muscles in her face were twitching as she tried to hold back what she knew was the inevitable. "My father will be here soon," she added.

Tom glanced quickly at his watch. "Unless he's doing one hundred twenty miles per hour, I wouldn't expect him for another half hour, at least."

"There is a distinct possibility he might do just that." She glanced over at him, saw the panic on his face and said, "Don't worry. He's a good driver."

"That's not what I was thinking. I'm not worried about the truck."

"Oh."

Her sneakers were still soaked and made a squishy suction sound on the polished floor as she paced. She glanced at the door behind which her son was now being cared for by doctors and nurses. She just needed a moment to catch her breath and she'd be back in there with him.

Breathe in. Breathe out.

It was times like this that her resentment toward Kent multiplied tenfold. He should be here with her, standing beside Brian. And if not with Brian, with her. But he'd never been. Even before his death. And now it was too late.

Jenna hugged her middle and turned to Tag. "What time is it?"

"About two forty-five in the morning."

She sighed, sat down on one of the chairs in the waiting room and pressed her hands to her tired eyes. The night had already been long and was getting longer. But sitting didn't calm her nerves the way it should, so she stood up again and paced. It gave her something to do, some way of draining the nervous energy flooding her.

"Hey, do you want me to go down to the cafeteria and get us some coffee or some—"

"The cafeteria is closed," she said quickly. "It won't open until about eight o'clock. If you want some coffee, I think there is a vending machine on the second floor, by Radiology, and maybe another one just outside the gift shop. I hear it's nasty, though."

Tom placed his hands gently on both of her shoulders, the contact surprising her. She peered up at him, only to be greeted by a warm smile. "I was asking for you."

She swallowed a gulp of air. And then another. "Oh, sure," she said and then nodded.

"Good. You're soaking wet, and you look like you're freezing. Maybe some hot chocolate will help warm you up."

Her bottom lip trembled violently as she watched him walk down the corridor to the vending machine. And without any more warning the floodgates opened.

Tag went stiff as he walked back into the waiting room with a cup of vending-machine hot chocolate in his hand. Jenna was sitting in a seat, leaning forward, with her face in her hands. Her shoulders rocked, as if she was crying.

How on earth…or rather, what on earth had happened in the few short minutes he'd been gone?

He set the hot chocolate down on the end table and quickly sat down next to Jenna, gently placing his hand on her back.

"What…happened?" he asked, a sudden panic

rising up in his throat as the possibilities raced through his mind.

Had the doctor come out with bad news about Brian?

He patted her back, the sudden closeness between them crowding in around him. Jenna continued to cry for a few minutes, before she sniffed a few times and sat back, shaking her head.

"Oh, I'm so sorry," she said, swiping at her cheeks with her fingers.

Tag placed a napkin in front of her. She quickly took it and began to dry her face.

"How awful of me. You don't even know me, and I'm blubbering like an idiot." And she began to cry again, covering her face with her hands. The sobs were softer now, but still heartbreaking.

Just when he thought she'd back away, she leaned in closer to him. Not knowing exactly how to comfort her, he draped an arm loosely on her shoulder. "It's okay. You're upset." Cautiously, he added, "Is Brian okay?"

Jenna's shoulders shook, and he braced himself for another round of heavy sobs. But when she lifted her head, she wasn't crying. She was sniffing and shaking her head at the same time.

"No news on Brian yet. That's not why I fell

apart. I really am sorry. I'm so embarrassed. I can't believe I did this in front of you, especially after you've been so kind tonight."

He quirked a smile, relieved he didn't have to deal with more tears for the moment. They'd only be his undoing.

"Yeah, well, my talents are many."

Jenna was truly a mess, Tag thought as he stared down at her. When she'd first appeared at his door earlier, he'd thought she looked like a mop. Now her matted hair was beginning to dry and frizz, her nose was red and her eyes puffy. With the rolled-up napkin, which was now soaked, she swiped at her wet cheeks and sniffed a few more times.

"Let me see if I can find you a box of Kleenex or a paper towel or—"

"A hose?" She laughed. "No, I'm fine. Really."

"You're sure?" Tag looked around the waiting room, wondering how long the doctor would take with Brian and how long it would take Ben to burn rubber with old faithful to get here. He was out of his league with this one. She clearly needed something he wasn't equipped to give. But the look on her face at the airport had been heartbreaking. The least he could do was stay with her until her father arrived.

Tag spotted a box of tissues on an end table on the other side of the waiting room and used that as an excuse to break away from the closeness with Jenna. He quickly retrieved the box and handed it to her.

Jenna looked up at him with an apologetic expression. "I feel I owe you an explanation. You must think I'm a truly horrible mother for not being in there with Brian."

"No. No, I don't. I think under the circumstances—"

"I should be with my son."

"Well…is there a reason you're not?"

She nodded and pulled out a tissue from the box he'd handed her. She blew her nose before saying anything else.

"Brian was born in Germany, so there was no family to come with me to the hospital, especially after my husband's death. From the time Brian was little, I was used to taking him to the hospital alone. Back then, I *would* stay with him the whole time, but it was hard. These last few months my father has come with me, and I guess I've let my guard down a little. I can usually manage to keep myself together long enough to get Brian here. But when we get here, and the doctors and nurses are working with him, all I see is my little baby and…I don't know. Lately, I've needed a moment to just fall to pieces before I get back to him. Dr. Healy says it's best for me to step outside and get myself together so I don't end up upsetting Brian more."

"Does your father stay out here with you?"

"No." She took a deep breath. "Dad usually goes in with Brian so he's not scared when I leave the room. That's why I've been okay taking this time. Except he's not here right now and I'm sure that made me more emotional. Even if it means leaving Brian alone with the doctors, I've gotten too used to having this time to be able to sit in there with Brian without crying."

"Your mother isn't around?"

She shook her head. "Mom passed away from breast cancer just after I got married. It's just the three of us now that my sister, Elaine, has moved away."

"What happened to Brian's father?"

"He passed away of the same disease Brian has. He was in the military, too, and when he pushed himself too hard on a training mission, he got sick."

"I'm sorry to hear that," he said quietly. "That must be tough on both of you."

"Brian was very young. He barely remembers his father, especially since he was gone so much."

"So you always stay out here by yourself?"

"I stay with Brian when we get to the hospital until the doctor is ready to see him. But as soon as they take him to X-ray or need to examine him fully, I slip outside so I can have my meltdown. It usually passes quickly, and then I can get right back to Brian." She smiled sheepishly. "When you gave me a minute to myself while you went to get a coffee…" She chuckled and hid her face with her hands.

It was beginning to make sense. Long nights, quiet corridors, intense fear. He knew a little too much about that. No wonder she needed some time to fall apart. Anyone would. The only problem he saw was that she had to put herself back together all alone.

"I'm used to dealing with things myself. I'm not used to having someone here to see what a mess I am." She glanced at the wet spot on his shirt. Reaching over, she lightly brushed her hand over the mark she'd left. A tingling sensation shot through him with the contact. "Or give me a shoulder to cry and slobber all over."

She pulled her hand away and an odd sensation began to stir there, making his insides hum.

"Anyway, thank you. For everything."

"It's okay."

Jenna pushed to her feet and wiped her face of residual tears. "I can't stand the thought of Brian in there alone. But I can't let him see me like this. I have to pull myself together."

"I can go check on him."

"No. You're a stranger, and as much as I'd like you to be my personal fly on the wall, I'm not even sure the doctor would let you in. Anyway, he's in good hands for now. Dr. Healy has been Brian's doctor since we moved back to Nebraska. Brian likes him a lot and trusts him. He'll be okay."

"I'm sure he will."

Jenna walked to the window, and as she did, she caught a glimpse of her reflection in the glass and cringed. Now was not the time for vanity, but she had to admit that she truly looked hideous. The wind and rain had blown her normally controlled hair into a wild mass of tangles. Her mascara had smudged under her eyes, making her look like a raccoon. The front of her shirt was wet and dirty from trying to help her father get the truck going before they finally abandoned it and decided to go for help.

She told herself it didn't matter what she looked like. Her only concern was her son's well-being. But as she turned and saw Tom Garrison sitting in the chair, hunched over with his elbows resting on his knees, her head began to swim. What a first impression she must have made! Whereas he had come out of the encounter looking like nothing less than a hero.

Under normal circumstances she would find the man very attractive. He didn't have the normal military buzz cut and instead had jet-black hair long enough for fingers to rake through. He'd combed it at some point between the time he'd opened his front door and now. His shoulders were as wide as he was tall, it seemed. And they were strong. She'd felt that firsthand.

She pulled her gaze away from him and flipped a lock of unruly hair behind her ear, telling herself again that it didn't matter what he *or* she looked like.

"You really don't need to stick around here if you don't want to," she finally said to him.

"It's okay. I can stay until your father gets here."

"You don't have to feel like you need to babysit me. You must be exhausted."

"I'm fine. I slept a little before you got to the

house. I don't want to leave you until you're sure you'll be okay."

She shook her head as she folded her arms across her chest. "I'm okay now, really. And Dad will be here soon. I think my episode is over. I'm going to go back into the room with Brian. Thank you so much for flying us here. And for the use of your truck. We'll drive it back as soon as we can. I hope it won't inconvenience you not to have it until tomorrow afternoon."

Tom shook his head. "Not a problem. I have a lot of work around the farm that will keep me busy. I won't even notice it missing."

She held out her hand, and he slipped his over hers, giving it a gentle squeeze.

"Thank you again for all your kindness."

She watched Tom walk away, and as he did, he glanced back once, giving her a quick smile that made her heart do a flip. Then she was alone.

Like always.

You're a scumbag, Garrison.

Tag strode through the automatic hospital doors, the moist air hitting him in the face, before he spun on his heels and waltzed back into the lobby. The need to bolt was overwhelming, but the guilt he felt in leaving Jenna alone was winning out.

*What kind of person leaves a vulnerable woman
alone in her time of need?*

"You do," he said aloud to himself and then
silently called himself a few choice words. He
stopped in the middle of the lobby, his fingers
tucked into the front pockets of his jeans, and
stared at the corridor leading to Emergency.

Sighing, he shook his head. He could still hear
the justifications running through his head. Ben
was going to be here any minute. There was absolutely no reason for him to stay any longer. Jenna
had even told him to go. It wasn't his problem. His
good deed for the day was done. Besides, what
comfort could he really be to her when they didn't
even know each other? She'd said it herself. He
was a stranger.

The words sounded real nice running through
his mind, and he was even willing to bet they'd
sound pretty good rolling off his tongue, too. But
Tag wasn't about to let himself off the hook that
easily. He'd never thought of himself as a man
who'd leave someone stranded—and yet he'd done
just that to his own family while in the military.

He needed to find a pay phone to call for a cab
to bring him back to the airport. He wouldn't stay.
He'd done his job by getting Brian to the hospital

quicker than if they'd driven the wet roads. His part in this was done.

But that wasn't the real reason he was running for the door. Jenna Atkins needed someone to be there for her. Her child was seriously sick and she needed someone. The woman was clearly in need of comfort and a hand to hold.

But he couldn't be that man. He'd never been there for the people who needed him the most, when he was needed the most. He'd taken the easy way out and left them to handle nights like this on their own.

They don't get any lower than you, bud.

It had been more than two years since he'd held Nancy. His heart squeezed just thinking about what he'd put her through.

Lord, help me, he thought as he spun around and started for the automatic doors again. *Lord, help her,* he amended. The Lord hadn't been part of his life in quite a while. It was another reason he should just forget about Jenna Atkins. A Christian woman didn't need a man like him.

He reached the doors in time to find Ben Atkins jogging through.

"How are my kids?" Ben said when he caught sight of Tag.

"Brian is with the doctor. Jenna is holding her

own. She had a bit of a meltdown, but she was going back to Brian when I left."

Relief washed over Ben's face. "Good. I can't thank you enough."

"There's time enough for thanks later. Your family needs you." *Jenna needs you.*

Tag didn't look back as he strode through the doors a second time. This time for good. He didn't need a cab. He'd walk back to the airport if it took till dawn. The rain would feel good, help wash away this nagging feeling he couldn't shake.

Jenna had her daddy now to help her through her tough time. He didn't have to stay behind and play the big hero for her, or for anyone else, for that matter, anymore.

Because the truth of it was, he was nobody's hero.

Chapter Three

The spring day had turned unseasonably hot. A bead of sweat nagged at Jenna's collarbone before joining another one in an unending journey beneath her white cotton shirt. It had been her bright idea to bake all day instead of spending it sewing. Hot weather always made her restless, unable to concentrate on her business, no matter how much work needed her attention. With Brian in the hospital, she'd lost the last three days of work and now had a mountain of sewing to do to catch up with orders.

Still, the good thing about owning your own company, no matter how small, was that you could make your own hours. This was especially useful now that she lived at the farm and had to balance helping her father with chores, giving Brian the attention he required for his medical needs and still making time to sew and take care of orders for her company.

Her mother had taught her to sew as a child. While living on base, Jenna had had difficulty finding clothes she liked where they were stationed, so she had designed and sewn her clothes herself. It had helped pass the time while Kent had been away on missions. Pretty soon the other military wives had taken notice and asked her to sew for them. Her little cottage industry had filled her quiet evenings and had given her a few extra pennies in her pocket to put away for decorating Brian's room before her baby was born.

After Kent died, she and Brian had moved to Omaha and Jenna had started Eye For Style. It started slowly, mostly with her old customers from the base, but as word of mouth spread, it grew. With Kent's military benefits and the modest amount she made from Eye For Style, Jenna had enough to live on and pay for Brian's treatment.

God had been good to her. She had always known that if she put in the effort, the Lord would provide. She was able to keep up with her bills and the stressful routine Brian needed for treatment. But living in the city, it soon became obvious that she wasn't a superwoman.

She'd stayed in the city as long as she could,

wanting to be closer to the state-of-the-art medical facilities for Brian. But her need for emotional support, and her father's difficulty with the farm after Jenna's mother died and her sister moved away, convinced her it was the right move to come back to her hometown of Chesterfield, Nebraska. She'd already established a few solid accounts that automatically bought her goods back in Omaha and on some of the military bases she'd lived on. They kept her busy enough that now she was actually backlogged with work. She just hadn't felt like doing it—not today.

There was time enough for her to sew and design later tonight. She could go home and shower off all this sweat from baking and sitting in a hot truck as she drove to the Nelson farm— no, make that Garrison's farm. No doubt she'd feel more settled once this errand was done.

She'd made a chicken potpie for him. She had no idea if Tom liked chicken potpie, but Jenna knew she cooked a good one, and she couldn't very well show up empty-handed when she returned his truck. She didn't know of a better way to thank him than to feed him. Since he'd admitted to living alone, she banked on him appreciating the home-cooked meal. It was the least she could do for all he'd done for them.

Her father had offered to return the truck upon their arrival home the morning after they'd taken Brian to Valentine, but Tom had said to keep it until Brian was out of the hospital.

Brian had stayed two days while Dr. Healy observed him. His fever spike had been just a symptom of one of those childhood bugs that kids get, he'd told Jenna. That might be so. But most parents didn't have to fear losing their child to the slightest illness like she did.

It would probably take her a few weeks to stop mother-henning Brian, as she always did after one of his episodes. Brian, on the other hand, had barely been out of the truck when he'd gone bouncing into the barnyard to see some new piglets that had arrived while he'd been gone.

As Jenna pulled onto the dirt driveway leading to the Garrison farmhouse, a nervous energy jumped to life beneath her skin. Her mouth went dry when she saw Tom heaving what looked like a fifty-pound bag of grain into his arms.

She glanced in the rearview mirror and discovered that her father and Brian weren't behind her. Quickly turning her head back toward the road, she found that they were nowhere in sight.

"Terrific," she growled. Jenna hit the steering wheel with the palm of her hand.

They'd pulled out right behind her when she'd left the farm. She hadn't been paying attention during her drive to notice that they'd probably only made it to the end of the driveway before something else happened to their truck. If she'd bothered to glance in the rearview mirror, she would have known they weren't behind her before she got too far and would have turned back home.

Reaching in her purse for her cell phone, she noticed she had no bars for service. Cell phone service in this part of Nebraska was spotty at best and near nonexistent in most of Chesterfield.

She couldn't exactly turn back now and find out what had happened. Tom had already spun around and recognized his own truck coming down the driveway, so there was nothing Jenna could do but keep on driving. She didn't want to appear rude and leave without an explanation.

A dry breeze whistled past the window and added to the tension that was mounting inside her.

You're being ridiculous, she told herself flatly, almost laughing aloud with nervous energy. *How many pies have you baked for new people in town? Tons. You've greeted lots of new neighbors in the years you've lived in Chesterfield and while living on base somewhere in the world.*

That might be so, but none of them looked as good in a pair of faded denims and a white cotton shirt stretched taut over muscles as he did.

Give him the chicken potpie, thank him for his kindness and then leave. Nothing to feel awkward about. Well, except for the walk home she had ahead of her. Now that she knew her father wasn't behind her, her sandals would make the mile-long walk back to her farm a little challenging.

The pickup rolled to a stop right in front of the spot where Tom was standing. Discarding the bag of grain that had been in his arms, he walked around the front of the truck and greeted her on the driver's side.

Grabbing the potpie, she eased out of the front seat and allowed Tom to shut the door behind her.

Tom glanced at the potpie and then at her. His eyebrows knitted before a slow smile tugged at the corners of his lips.

Jenna thrust the potpie out at him. "I brought back the truck."

As he took in the situation, his face quickly registered alarm. "What did you do to it?"

"Excuse me?"

Nodding to the chicken potpie, he said, "If

you have to butter me up with food, then I figure you've got something bad to tell me."

Her cheeks flamed. "No, nothing happened. The potpie is just a…thank-you."

She saw appreciation creep into the smooth amusement that replaced his panicked expression.

"By the smell of it, I'd say it's home cooked and…chicken?"

"Chicken potpie, to be exact."

He nodded and leaned over to take a closer sniff of the still hot food, which she held with pot holders.

"I figured working all day, you probably don't have time to cook for yourself," she added.

"Actually, I kinda like cooking for myself. It helps me wind down a little after a hard day's work."

Her shoulders sagged. "Oh."

"But since I'm really not all that great a cook, I can almost guarantee you that anything you cook would taste a whole lot better than what I can put together. It already smells better than my best attempts. That's why I'm always grateful when someone else does the cooking."

She smiled.

He looked into the truck and then down the

driveway. "Are Brian and your father coming in a little while?"

She sighed, feeling more heat creep up her cheeks. "They were supposed to be right behind me. I had good intentions of bringing back your truck and then leaving with them so you could enjoy your dinner, but…"

"Your truck broke down again," he concluded.

"Most likely."

"Then I guess it's just you and me for dinner. More chicken potpie for us."

She absorbed his words and felt a new surge of embarrassment as she realized how it might look to him. Did he think she'd set this up to wrangle an invite to share his dinner? She hadn't dated since Kent died, and she wasn't looking for a date now.

"Oh, I wasn't inviting myself over for dinner. This dinner was for you. I was just going to drop it by and leave. In fact, if you're still busy, I can leave it in your oven to warm. It'll be ready for you when you're ready to eat."

"I'm always ready for chicken potpie. You don't expect me to eat this thing alone, do you? I've got a big appetite, but this is too big even for me to eat by myself."

Jenna had the feeling he was just trying to be nice. Just what she needed. A nice guy. She'd always had a soft spot for nice guys. If she could have covered her face with her hands, she would have. But she was still holding the chicken potpie.

"This looks so bad."

Tom chuckled, and she decided she really liked the sound of his laughter, the deep sound of his voice and the way his eyes brightened to a sparkling blue.

"What's worse is me eating this whole potpie alone. And by the smell of it, I can see me doing just that. It's too good not to share. Besides, I don't bite, Jenna."

"No, I know that, but—"

"No buts. Having dinner with you is certainly more appealing than what I had planned for tonight."

"Which was what? I don't want to keep you from your plans."

"That's just it. I didn't have any. And I probably would have planned dinner by what I found in the cupboards, which are kinda bare just now. Look, there's plenty here. We could drive over to your place and all have dinner together there, if you like."

"They've probably already eaten. I made a potpie for us, too, before we left and left it warming in the oven." She glanced at her watch. "Dad's stomach runs like clockwork. I'm sure he was pretty ticked off when the truck broke down again. He probably abandoned it for the hot food he knew was keeping in the oven."

Tom nodded and stared at her. "I don't blame him. Why don't we go inside and dig into this one? I don't know how long I can stand to just smell it. I can drive you home afterwards."

"No, you don't have to do that. Our farm is only a little ways up the road."

"You just said the truck probably broke down again."

"Yeah, and given its age, and the various knee patches my father has already added to it, it'll probably take all night for him to get it started again."

Tom simply nodded. "That good a track record, huh?"

"Lately. It was pretty dependable up until recently."

"It's a nice night for a walk, but those don't really look like the best shoes for it. Besides, if your dad and Brian dig into their potpie at home, you probably won't have a morsel left for you by the time you get there."

She laughed at the image of Brian and her father devouring the chicken potpie. "You're probably right. You sure it's no trouble?"

"Hey, you're the one who made dinner." He smiled at her with amusement. "Let's dig into this and then see what we can do about the truck."

She wasn't in the market for a relationship with any man. Especially a military man, however far removed from active duty Tom was at the present time. Her late husband had given her plenty of reason to be gun-shy in that regard.

Jenna followed Tom into the house, he carrying the potpie with pot holders and she fiddling with her hands for lack of something to do with them. The screen door slammed behind her, making her jump as she walked into the house.

Unlike her kitchen, Tom's kitchen was cool. But then his oven hadn't been working overtime today, baking chicken potpies and cookies for Brian's homecoming.

"Would you like a glass of iced tea?" he asked, setting the pie plate on the counter and walking over to the refrigerator to grab a full pitcher of tea already prepared.

"Yes, thanks." When he set only one glass on the counter, she added. "Aren't you having any?"

"In a bit." He turned to her and said, "You know, I've got a grunge thing happening here from being outside all day. Right now I'm bordering on truly offensive. It might be a good idea if I take a minute to clean up before we eat. Do you mind? You're not in a hurry, are you?"

"No, that's fine. I can keep the food warm in the oven."

"Don't go anywhere."

"I'll be right here."

Needing something to do after Tom left the kitchen, she leaned against the counter and looked around, crossing her arms over her chest. She was normally comfortable in a kitchen, but she didn't know what to do with herself here in Tom's. She took a moment to call her house to make sure her father and Brian had made it home okay, which they had, but after that, she was at loose ends again.

With the sound of running water filtering in from the other room, Jenna decided to make use of her time and began searching cabinets for some plates, napkins and silverware to set the table.

The local newspaper was folded neatly on the table along with some mail. One letter was open and sat on top. Before she could scoop it up from the table, she noticed the official Department of Defense seal at the top. She'd seen that seal before, and it immediately brought back to mind the official letter she'd received after Kent died on a training mission. Tom may be out of active duty but he wasn't so far removed that they couldn't find him.

Since it wasn't any of her business, she left the letter on top of all the mail and tucked the pile neatly away on the corner of the counter for Tom to deal with later.

A few minutes later she'd found most of what she needed to set the table. She hadn't found any napkins so she'd settled instead for paper towels, which she'd found hanging from a roll by the sink. She looked at the table and decided it would do.

By the time she'd poured a fresh glass of iced tea for herself and then one for Tom, she heard the water turn off in the bathroom. Jenna was contemplating the fact that she should have remembered to bring a loaf of French bread or a salad to serve with dinner when Tom stepped into the kitchen, making her jump.

He'd shaven. She couldn't figure out how he'd moved so fast, washing all the dirt and grime from his hands and face and managing to shave

his five o'clock shadow, too, but he had. He had
changed into clean clothes and now wore a pair
of army fatigues and a plain white T-shirt.

"Wow, I see you found what little I had for the
table."

"I hope you don't mind. I moved your mail to
the counter so we wouldn't get any food stains on
important papers."

Tom picked up the top letter with the Department of Defense seal and glanced at her, then
back at the stack of mail. He quickly stuffed the
letter into the empty envelope and said, "Thanks.
It all looks great. I hope you didn't have to do any
washing up. Usually, only one plate gets used at
a time. The rest might be a little dusty."

"You don't have much company?"

"I just moved here. I don't know anyone."

"You know me."

"I'm getting there."

Her insides hummed in a way she hadn't felt
for quite some time. His startling blue eyes locked
onto hers, and she actually felt her hands begin to
sweat.

"I don't want the potpie to get cold," she said,
deliberately breaking the mood.

He didn't look away while he pulled a chair
from the table and waited for her to sit in it.

A gentleman. Or a gentle man. Either way, it was flattering to have a man treat her like a lady again after all this time. For that matter, it was nice to simply share a meal with a man—to have the sense that he welcomed her company and was pleased to spend time with her.

Kent had been like that once, when they'd first met. She'd been a nineteen-year-old college student, swept off her feet by his charm and his obvious interest in her. Giving up college and taking on the nomadic life of a military wife had been a choice she'd made willingly out of love. She'd later found out Kent didn't make such sacrifices for love, especially when he'd made the choice to reenlist soon after Brian's diagnosis. The military had given him an excuse to ignore what he didn't want to face the fact that he wasn't capable of being someone she could depend on.

Looking back, their marriage had ended long before his death during that training mission. His death had just highlighted their problems. "A freak accident," the commander had called it, but Jenna knew the truth. Kent had ignored the symptoms of his illness until he faltered because of it, causing his plane to crash. The autopsy had revealed a ruptured kidney cyst, the most likely cause of the accident.

Jenna had been left a widow at the very young age of twenty-three.

Alone and with a sick baby, it was her faith in God that had given her the support she'd never gotten from her husband when she needed it. She'd also learned to depend on herself. Independence was her motto now, especially when it came to caring for her son.

If Tom had noticed the faraway place she'd been in in her mind, he didn't say. He simply sat down opposite Jenna at the small round table in the center of the kitchen, respecting her need to take a moment for her thoughts. Finally, though, the silence grew awkward. She struggled for something to say.

"Did you grow up around here?" Tom asked at the same moment she asked, "Do you have family from Chesterfield?"

His awkward smile matched the way she felt, and oddly put her at ease.

"I grew up here," she said quickly. "My parents inherited the farm from my mother's parents. I still have the same bedroom I had when I was five."

"Complete with Barbie doll wallpaper?"

"How'd you know?" she teased.

His smile widened, and Jenna decided it was

worth it to stand in a hot kitchen and sweat all day just to come by here and see that smile.

"Your turn," she said, placing a helping of potpie on his dish and handing it to him.

"Like I said, I don't know anyone here."

"Chesterfield isn't exactly a hopping metropolis. In fact, it isn't even on most maps. How'd you find this place?"

"I needed a change, opened up a map, closed my eyes and stuck my finger down on the paper. Where my finger landed is where I ended up."

She set down her fork. "Really?"

He nodded.

"Wow, I could never be that spontaneous."

"It really wouldn't have mattered where I went. But do you know what I thought of the first time I drove into Chesterfield?"

She shook her head.

"This place is quiet."

She laughed then. "Not around my house. I have a seven-year-old boy."

Tom wasn't laughing, though. He was just looking at her, through her.

"You like the quiet?" she finally asked when it became too uncomfortable.

"Yeah, it's nice." He took a bite of the potpie and nodded. "This is good."

"Thank you."

"I've missed good food."

"You don't like your own cooking?"

"For some reason, it always tastes better when someone else cooks."

"We'll have to have you over for dinner sometime. That is, if you're ever looking to get away from all this quiet."

She wondered for a fleeting moment if she'd said the wrong thing. It was her nature to be neighborly. Chesterfield and its farms had wide borders, and you weren't likely to get chitchat at the mailbox at the end of the driveway, but her house—and many others in the area—had an open door. There was always another place set at the table, be it for someone who'd come out to the farm to help her father or for one of Brian's friends from school.

They ate most of their meal in awkward silence mixed with small talk. Unlike Tom, Jenna knew almost everyone in Chesterfield and was only too willing to answer his questions about the town, if only to keep the conversation going. After a while, it became easier and she relaxed until the questions turned to Brian's health.

"We make the trip out to Valentine three times

a week for dialysis," Jenna said. "More, if we have an incident like the other night."

"Three times a week is a haul for both of you."

"You said it. But it's necessary. I usually schedule the trips after school so Brian doesn't miss schoolwork. It would be easier if the clinic in town was set up for dialysis, but it doesn't have the funds for the equipment. There isn't a need for them to spend the money just for one person, so Brian and I commute. Unfortunately, our one truck has taken a beating because of it. I can't tell you how many times I've gotten caught by the side of the road. I know just about everyone en route from here to Valentine."

He simply nodded, scraped the plate clean of the last remnants of the chicken potpie. "This was good. Certainly better than what I had planned for tonight."

She smiled. "Any further thought on what that would have been?"

"I probably would have ended up eating a bowl of cereal."

Tom insisted she sit and relax while he cleared the dishes and put them in soapy water to soak. Afterward, they sat on the back porch with bowls of vanilla ice cream to top off dinner, and then he drove her home. The ride was made in silence, except for the night creatures calling out as they drove by.

Her father's old truck was parked in front of the house, with tools strewn about on the ground around it. It was clear that what she'd already suspected was true. The truck was dead. The hood was still up, a clear indication there hadn't been success as yet in fixing whatever was wrong with it. A quick glance showed her father was nowhere to be found.

Tag parked right behind Ben's truck. He got out of the driver's seat and walked over to the beat-up truck, which he was sure had seen better days than this. He glanced down at the dark stains on the dirt and the pan under the truck that was catching liquid.

"It's leaking oil something fierce," he said. "How long has it been doing that?"

"Awhile."

"Looks like you've got a blown gasket."

Jenna chuckled. "I'll take your word for it."

He scrutinized the truck. "When's Brian's next appointment?"

She sighed and closed her eyes. Her blush crept up her cheeks, making her skin glow. "It's very nice of you to offer your truck again," she said, guessing the direction he was going. "But I can't keep relying on your generosity. We've been putting off buying another truck for some time. Now it looks like we're just going to have to break down and do it. I can't risk taking Brian back and forth if I can't trust this truck, even if I have come to know a lot of people along the way from here to Valentine."

He nodded. "You might be able to get this one running enough to do errands around town, but I agree it's not safe to keep taking it to Valentine a couple of times a week."

He glanced around their farm. It was in better shape than his for sure, but times were tough and there wasn't always a lot of extra money at the end of the month to put toward a car payment and high insurance.

"I don't think I told you before, but the first person I met when I came to town was Decker Peers," he added.

"Mr. Peers? He must have talked your ear off about everyone in town. He knows everyone."

Tag smiled. "Yes, he does, and he was quick to let some of the other businesses in town know I had a plane. Since he owns the only convenience store in the area and knows a lot of the other business owners, he offered to pay me to fly out to Valentine and pick up supplies to keep the shelves stocked, and to pick up special orders for him and the others. It's a lot easier for them to pick up inventory out at my farm than to run into Valentine to get everything themselves. Between Mr. Peers and a few of the other business owners he talked to, it looks like I'll be flying out a few times a week. I could coordinate my supply run with Brian's dialysis and bring you both."

"No," she said. "That's not necessary. You've got so many other people who need your services. What if the clinic needs you to make another flight out for a medical emergency?"

He smiled. "You must have been talking to Sheriff Johnson."

She shrugged. "He likes the idea of having a plane in town in case someone needs a life flight out to Valentine if the clinic can't handle a big emergency. Chesterfield has never had something like that before."

"I'm happy to do it, if I can. But that's for sudden emergencies. What you need is different. Since I have to go to Valentine, anyway, you're not putting me out of my way. And flying will make the trip quicker for both of you. The drive alone has got to be draining. This way you'll knock nearly two hours off your travel time each day. And you won't have to sit in traffic."

"I've already caused you so much trouble."

"Yeah, I had a whole lot of trouble downing that chicken potpie," he said with a chuckle. "There's really no reason why we can't enjoy each other's company and kill two birds with one stone."

"You won't miss all that *quiet?*"

A smile tugged at his lips. "I don't know," he answered honestly. "I have gotten used to flying alone."

He saw her working things around in her mind. All through dinner he'd been watching her, noticing how very different she looked today than she had the night they'd met. With all the worry washed away, she was a pretty woman. Her dark hair was pulled back with combs, and the dress she wore flowed around curves that had been hidden beneath that rain slicker.

He went on. "I tell you what. Why don't we just take things one trip at a time and see how it goes? Agreed?"

Tag had been prepared for her to be relieved with his offer. He couldn't stand to see all that worry on her face when she talked about Brian. He wasn't prepared for the tears that sprang to her eyes or the musical laugh that floated out of her mouth.

"Brian will love that!" she said.

Abruptly, she stepped forward and threw her arms around him, giving him a squeeze. When she pulled back, the look on her face told him she was just as surprised as he was by her impulsive gesture.

"Well," he said, for lack of something better to say.

While he knew his hands were shaking, Jenna merely laughed. That slight blush that had made her glow earlier crept up her cheeks again.

"I'd better go in before I make an even bigger fool of myself," she said, the smile never leaving her lips.

Jenna turned and ran into the house, her feet hitting the porch steps in time with the beating of Tag's heart. And he wondered what was more foolish. Wanting to chase her down for another hug or wanting to run like a bandit in the opposite direction?

Chapter Four

The weather was kind to them and the sky was a clear blue, which had Tag wanting to play. There were days like this when he wanted to spend the entire day in the air, just flying to places he hadn't yet seen. In his life he'd been blessed to be able to see new places, experience new things and meet new people, a fact that others could only dream about. The adventure never got old.

Joining the marines had been the right move for him when he was young. It had given him what he craved: the opportunity to serve his country, to help those around the world who couldn't help themselves and to live his dream. During the twelve years he'd served in the Marine Corps, he'd had his share of all of the above.

But living his dream had come with a price that others had paid. That realization had come too late for him. If he could go back... No, that wasn't possible. It was best to keep his mind on where he was at now.

Since the day he'd had dinner with Jenna, he'd wondered if she'd read that letter from the Department of Defense, proudly advising him that they had recognized his service to his country and wanted to award him the Medal of Honor for his heroic actions in Afghanistan.

Yeah, right. Heroic. Tag was no hero, and he didn't want any medal. He'd just done what he had to do. He didn't need a medal to remind him of anything.

If Jenna had seen it, she hadn't said anything. For that he was glad.

This was the third run taking Jenna and Brian to Valentine this week. In truth, he could have made the full run for the week's supplies for Mr. Peers and the other business owners in one trip, but with two passengers on board, even as light as Jenna and Brian were, he couldn't add more weight to the plane. And he certainly didn't mind the excuse to make more flights and spend more time in the air.

But it was more than that that had him enjoying the flights. He'd always loved flying alone, but Brian's chattiness and excitement were infectious.

"What does this one tell you?" Brian said, leaning forward against the restraint of the belt and pointing to the instrument panel.

"It tells you whether you're ascending or descending," Tag replied.

"What about that one?" Brian pointed to another dial.

"That's the ammeter. It blinks to tell you whether or not the engine or battery is getting enough juice. It reminds me if I don't have enough electricity."

"Electricity for what?" Brian asked.

"To run all the parts of the plane and keep it flying in the air."

Brian's eyes grew wide. "What if it starts blinking?"

Tag smiled mischievously. "Then we're in trouble." To Jenna he said, "But it's not blinking, so you can breathe."

Jenna gave him an amused grin.

It was the same every time they flew. Brian had a thousand and one questions for him about everything from the controls on the plane to what Tag did in the military. Jenna just sat back and let Brian chatter. But when they talked… Yeah, Tag realized he liked Jenna's company, too.

These last months he'd spent a fair amount of

time alone, just with himself. He'd needed that right after he returned from Afghanistan. He'd had to right himself when his life was spinning out of control. When there wasn't anyone else around, he didn't have to answer questions or disappoint anyone by not being social.

Jenna and Brian kept up more than their fair share of the social part, making things easier.

Lately the quiet he'd craved seemed less peaceful and more like noise in his head than thoughts that needed working out. He missed having someone to run ideas by, to talk to about the nonsense of life, and just plain sharing a meal. It had been so glaringly obvious that first night, when Jenna's truck broke down in his driveway.

And he missed a challenge. In the military there had always been some mission or project that gave him that challenge. But there was also a challenge in friendships. Tag had pushed a fair amount of his friendships away because they always turned back to his reason for leaving the military. The only one who still called was his cousin Wolf, and it would be only a matter of time before he stopped as well. But no. Wolf was family, and family had a way of never giving up.

Brian's voice broke into his thoughts just as the

plane bobbed with a bit of turbulence. Tag adjusted the plane's position to stabilize the ride.

"Are we going to crash, Tom?"

Tag glanced over his shoulder at Brian, who was sitting next to Jenna in the back row. His eyes were wide with panic as he pointed to another dial that was moving.

"Gee, I don't know, Brian. I hope you brought a parachute."

"Are we really going to have to jump out of the plane?" Brian's wide eyes darted to Tag, then to Jenna. The plane bobbed again, and Brian gripped the seat.

"Niiice," Jenna said, eyeing Tag with an amused warning. "Are you going to come over and talk him down from this ledge you're building for him when he has a nightmare tonight?"

Tag mouthed the word *sorry* and then turned to Brian. "Don't worry about it, Scout. It's just the directional indicator. If you noticed, I turned the plane just a little because we hit a few small air pockets that made the plane jump a bit. There's a bunch of those air pockets all over the sky, and we never know when we're going to hit them. But when we do, I can turn the plane until all the bumpiness from the air pocket stops. That's when I know we're clear. Think of it as being on a big roller coaster. You've been on a roller coaster before, right?"

Brian shook his head. "Only the little one. I'm too small for a big roller coaster."

"Big or small, it's kind of the same thing. Only when you're on a roller coaster, you can see the big hill coming. You just can't see the drop until you're there. That dial shows the pitch of the plane when I turn and then straighten out again. That's why you saw it moving just now."

Brian gave a quick smile. "I like roller coasters. Even the little ones. But Mom usually screams."

Tag laughed. "No screaming allowed in this plane."

Jenna rolled her eyes. "So noted."

"So we're not going to crash?" Brian asked.

"Tom was just having fun with you, sweetie," Jenna said, rumpling her son's hair.

Brian tried to peer out the window and look down at the ground, but his small size made it hard to see all the way down. "Did you ever have to jump out of a plane, Tom?" he asked.

"Yeah, plenty of times."

Brian's jaw dropped open wide. "Really? Like, from up this high and everything?"

"Sure. We used to do maneuvers like that all the time in the military. Sometimes we jumped from the plane and parachuted into a location. But most of the time we made drops into the jungle from a Super Stallion."

"That's one of those hover helicopters, right?" Jenna asked.

"Yeah, the Super Stallions can hover right above the tree line so a unit can rappel to the ground quickly. No parachutes." Tag winked at Brian, who finally eased into a smile.

The small landing strip in the center of his property came into view, and Tag's heart fell just a notch as he prepared to circle around to come in for a landing. Mr. Peers's truck sat waiting to be loaded with the supplies Tag had on board.

Calm winds made landing between the barren crop fields as easy as walking. But there was never anything routine about coming in for a landing. Tag stopped the chatter and gave landing the plane his full attention.

As the wheels hit the ground, a tug of disappointment washed over him. He loved flying, and he always felt a little sadness when his time in the air was over, but that sadness was stronger now that the end of a flight meant saying goodbye to Jenna and Brian.

"Are you eating dinner at our house, Tom?"

Brian said, already unbuckling his seat belt and getting up to kneel in the seat to see better.

His mother shooed him down, and Tag wasn't sure whether it was because he'd prematurely taken off the belt or because the boy had spoken out of turn, asking him to dinner.

Jenna had asked him to dinner herself the first two times he'd flown them, and he'd declined. He wasn't exactly sure why, since it took only a few minutes to load Mr. Peers's truck with the goods he brought back from Valentine. But somehow it felt more appropriate. The woman was sweet, and Chesterfield was a small town. Tag didn't want people coming to the conclusion that they were an item.

He was happy to have Jenna as a friend, but there was no room in his life for a romantic relationship or small talk from people who didn't know him or his history. They'd have to stay just friends. But then, was there really any reason why he couldn't have dinner with a friend? The food was guaranteed to be good and he knew he'd enjoy himself. Jenna was easy to be with and had a sunshine quality that made him smile.

"Your mom hasn't asked," he said.

"She's going to, though," Brian said resolutely. "She even said that she's going to insist this time, 'cuz she doesn't like getting things for free and she needs to pay you for your services."

"Brian!" Jenna exclaimed.

"But, Mom, you said so at breakfast!"

Tag couldn't help but laugh. "She said that, huh? Well, then, I guess a home-cooked dinner would go a long way toward payment." He glanced over his shoulder and saw that Jenna's cheeks had turned crimson. "That is, if it's okay with you, Jenna."

"I didn't say it like that," she said, touching her hand to her cheek and sighing. "Kids."

Tag glanced over his shoulder again and smiled at her.

"Honestly, if you don't have other plans, we'd love to have you," she said.

"It'd be my pleasure. I just need to unload some things here for Mr. Peers. And I've got those parts Ben wanted for the truck. Maybe Ben and I will have some time to work on the truck after dinner and get it running smoother."

He secured the plane and walked them back to his house, where she'd left her truck. Mr. Peers met them halfway.

"I'll be right with you, Mr. Peers," Tag said after they greeted each other.

Tag wanted to make sure Jenna's truck started

up without a problem. They'd managed to get the truck running, but it still ran rough. The new parts should solve the problem they'd been having so they didn't have to worry each time they took the truck out of the driveway. When the engine turned over, he nodded.

"I'll stop by the house and drop off the parts when I'm done here. If you're not home by the time I get there, I'll assume you broke down and come find you."

"You take too good care of me, Tom Garrison," she said, putting the truck into gear and then checking to make sure Brian had buckled up.

"How else am I going to get some home-cooked food?"

He watched Jenna drive away, suddenly aware that something had changed. He'd been living on the farm for a few weeks, but today was the first day that he felt he had the makings of a home here in Chesterfield. He was sure the woman driving away had something to do with it.

When Jenna had reached the end of the driveway, Tag turned back toward the plane to help Mr. Peers unload his supplies.

"Can I help Grandpa and Tom work on the truck after dinner, Mom?"

Jenna held Brian's hand as they crossed Main Street and walked toward Alice McKenna's house, which was near the center of town. Alice's son David was in Brian's class, and she had offered to have Brian over for the afternoon to play.

"Mom!"

Startled by Brian's outburst, she said, "What is it?"

"Can I?"

"Can you what?"

"Help Tom and Grandpa after dinner? He's coming over for dinner, isn't he?"

"You've got homework."

"I can finish it before then."

She was distracted for a moment as she mentally went over the menu she'd selected for dinner that night. Brian wasn't a picky eater, and her dad would eat just about anything she put in front of him. But since Tom was coming over, she thought she'd make something special.

"Mom?" Brian looked up at her impatiently.

"You can barely see above the hood of the truck. Won't you be bored?"

Stupid question. Male bonding rituals started young. Looking inside a truck with twisted metal parts and grease wasn't her thing, but since it involved his two heroes, Brian was bound to find it interesting. Whatever they were doing he just wanted to be with the guys. At any rate, she knew he wasn't going to give up easily. Her son never did when he had his mind fixed on something.

"I can stand on a hay bale."

Jenna chuckled, trying to squash the slight pang of jealousy that hit her. First a playdate and now she was competing for her son's attention with Tom. Not being the center of Brian's world was a new thing she was going to have to get used to.

It was going to be a busy afternoon for Brian and a long evening with Tom stopping by later. Normally Jenna would try to keep Brian to a schedule. But Brian was probably going to come up with a counterargument for everything she put in front of him.

She finally conceded, "If you get your homework done, then okay. But only as long as Grandpa and Tom say it's okay. And only until it's time for your bath. No going out there after you're clean."

Alice was at her front door when they made it up the walkway. Though it had been more than a decade since they'd gone to high school together, the pretty blonde looked much the same. Alice had graduated a few years before Jenna, and they hadn't been friends. Still, now that she was back in Chesterfield and the two of them had sons the same age, Jenna was looking forward to getting to know Alice better.

After Brian bustled through the door, Alice leaned forward and said quietly, "Anything I should watch out for?"

Jenna had mentioned Brian's dialysis treatments to Alice, so she was aware of his illness. "Keep the cookies to a minimum. Brian told me about the snickerdoodles David brings for lunch, and he said they were awesome." She mimicked the way Brian said it, and Alice laughed.

"David loves them, too. I'll make sure he has only a few."

"Good," Jenna said, smiling. "I'll never get him down from the sugar high otherwise. And if you can get him to drink some juice or lemonade, that'd be good, too. He never drinks enough. I'll be back in an hour or so to pick him up."

"Oh, that's okay. I can drive him home. That way you won't have to rush your errands. Is six o'clock okay?"

"That'd be great."

An afternoon to herself. This was something new.

She said her goodbyes and headed back the way she'd come. She'd have plenty of time to do her shopping before calling her father to come pick her up in town.

She knew her dad would welcome Brian's company later on, while working on the truck, even if Brian managed to get into something he wasn't supposed to when no one was looking. She was glad that the move back to Chesterfield had given Brian and her father an opportunity to have a closer relationship than they'd had when she and Brian had lived in Omaha. Sure, her dad gave in to every little thing Brian wanted, much to Jenna's dismay. But he was also a strong male influence, which Brian needed in his life right now.

Then there was Tom. In the short time she'd known him, Jenna had come to rely on his help and, yeah, even his friendship, despite the fact that he was very guarded with her. With Brian, however, Tom seemed to be an open book, and it was a refreshing side of him to see. He was genuine in his motives and never expected anything in return for a good deed.

Tom didn't need to come over to fix her truck. But she didn't have to ask him to do it, either. He just did it. And Jenna liked the feeling of having a man be attentive to the little things that way, wanting to help fix problems instead of running away from them.

If Tom stuck around long enough, she was sure she'd quickly get used to the feeling. It was a dangerous thought.

Jenna had just finished picking up the last vegetables needed for her roast dinner and was walking out of the market, bags filling her arms, when she saw Tom walking through the door of the hardware store next door.

"I'm glad I caught you," he said, turning back in her direction.

A momentary sense of disappointment hit her square in the stomach. "You're still coming for dinner, aren't you?"

"Sure, I'll be there. I just wanted to warn you your dad might not be in the best of moods."

She stopped walking and groaned. "Why?"

"The piece he ordered for the truck doesn't fit."

"Oh, no. Serves me right for talking him into saving a few pennies with an aftermarket part when the store didn't have the dealer part he was looking for."

Tom shrugged. "It was worth a shot. Sometimes it works out. Just not this time."

Jenna's shoulders sagged, but not from the weight of the groceries. "Can it be returned?"

"Your dad still has the receipt, so I can do that the next time we fly to Valentine for Brian's treatment," Tag said.

"That'd be great. I can call ahead and have the auto parts store hold the new part there until then."

Of course, that meant a wait of a few days. Her father no doubt was in a sour mood about that, too. She could almost see him pulling his hat off his head and brushing his silver hair back in frustration. The image that flashed in her mind reminded her that her father was getting older. The last few years had taken their toll on him. He was getting tired, and from what Tom said, he was no doubt grumpy because so much of the work he'd planned had been put on hold while he waited for the truck to be fixed.

Jenna wished it could be different. Her moving to Chesterfield had made some things easier on both of them to some degree, but it had made other things harder. The wear and tear she'd added to the truck was only part of it.

"Thanks for warning me," she said.

"I figured I should. He's really disappointed," Tom said.

"I'm sure that's putting it mildly. There's a whole lot of work piling up around here, and he needs that truck to get it done."

"I offered to take him into town to get the supplies he needs. He can even borrow—"

"Your truck?" She smiled and felt her cheeks heat up. "It bothers him that he has to ask for help."

"He didn't ask. I offered. Having a second set of arms to load the truck with supplies will make the job go quicker, too. Speaking of load, why don't you let me take those?"

"Thanks." She handed him one of the packages.

"Where is Brian?" he asked, looking around.

"He's at a playdate with a friend from school. He's going to be dropped off around dinnertime."

"Oh, then you're out playing in town on your own?"

Jenna chuckled. "Yeah, if you can call grocery shopping playing."

"Why don't we head across the street and have an ice cream cone at the café. I hear it's really good."

She smirked. "Dessert before dinner?"

"Live on the wild side, Jenna. I promise I won't tell."

With a shrug of her shoulder, she said, "Why not? It's not often I have a free afternoon."

"That's the spirit."

Tom's truck was parked outside the hardware store. He stowed her grocery bags in the truck before they ran across the street to the Freeze Factory, an ice cream parlor she'd gone to many times as a child. They ordered two double chocolate ice cream cones—hers with rainbow sprinkles—and sat at an outside table, watching the downtown Chesterfield traffic go by.

When Tom broached the subject of borrowing his truck again, stating it was not charity to borrow a friend's car, Jenna braced herself, trying to find the right words that would make him understand her father's resistance.

"I hear what you're saying, but it still feels like charity to him," she said delicately. "You don't know my father. He hates depending on other people. He was independent for so long. It bothers him now that he can't handle everything himself. Whether my father likes to admit it or not, he can't take on the same workload he did when he was twenty."

"I don't know about that. I've seen him lift quite a hefty load. He's still pretty fit. And he has a lot of energy in him with Brian."

Jenna smiled. "Brian brings out the best in him. It's one of the many reasons why I'm glad we moved here."

She closed her eyes for a brief moment as the spring breeze blew her hair forward. This was Jenna's favorite time of the year. Looking around, she saw that the crocuses that Mrs. Shasta had planted years ago had come and gone and only a handful of bright yellow daffodils remained in narrow boxed flower beds snug up against the ice cream parlor. Somewhere there was a lilac tree still blooming. She recalled it was her mother's favorite flower, and Jenna made a mental note to visit the nursery in town to see if there were any lilac trees still in stock. She knew the perfect place to plant one on the farm would be right outside the kitchen window.

If you grew up in Chesterfield, you either stayed or you left for bigger and better things. Jenna had left and come home, feeling more battered by life than she cared to admit.

Now she was with Tom. It had been a long time since Jenna had enjoyed the companionship of a man, and she decided she liked it. It had been missing from her life for quite some time.

It wasn't until Tom spoke that she realized she'd been lost in her own thoughts.

"Where'd you go?"

A warm blush crept up her cheeks. "Just

thinking." Looking around, she added, "I never realized how much I missed Chesterfield until I came home."

"I think I understand why. Chesterfield is a nice town."

A warm feeling spread through her with his appreciation of what they had here.

An older-model sedan with a teenage couple pulled in to a parking space in front of the table they were sitting at. The young couple got out of the car, holding hands, and walked into the ice cream parlor. The young girl looked dreamily at her boyfriend, making Jenna remember what it was like to be that young.

She smiled wistfully before turning her attention back to Tom. He was at ease. Some of the rough edges she'd noticed when they first met had smoothed out. His comfort level had reached a good point, where she didn't feel like he was always ready to bolt when he was around her.

"You know, I have to say I'm surprised you chose Chesterfield. Being in the military, you must have traveled the world at lightning speed. Country living doesn't seem too slow-paced for you?"

"Yeah, I've traveled, but I wouldn't call myself a world traveler. And it was the slower pace that drew me to Chesterfield. My love of being in the country comes from my experiences in childhood, and the military."

"Really?"

"After growing up in the suburbs, I found I liked wide open spaces. Since I'm an only child, I spent a lot of time as a kid with my cousin Wolf. We're about the same age, and the two of us used to go out to the lakes every chance we got with Oma and Opa." At her confused expression, he added, "Our grandparents. They grew up in Germany and came over to America after World War II. Opa lived on a farm back in Germany and liked the outdoors, so he took us camping a lot. Then when I was in the marines, I spent a lot of time in the jungle, the swamps."

Jenna made a face. "Gee, sounds fun."

He laughed. "Actually, I didn't mind it. The bugs were killers, but if you were prepared, that was okay, too. I loved the sound of the night and having nature all around me."

"Well, I tell you what. You and Brian can trade bug stories at dinner. I'm sure he'd enjoy that."

"I'd be happy to talk bugs as much as Brian wants. He's probably found some interesting ones around here. I wish I'd grown up in a place like

Chesterfield. Wolf and I would have spent a whole lot more time exploring."

She quirked an eyebrow. "Something tells me you really mean getting into trouble."

He laughed. "Probably. But this really is a great place for kids to just get to know nature. It's clear that Brian loves it. I'm surprised it took you so long to move back here."

A familiar stab of pain pierced her. "I wanted to be closer to the medical facilities in the city."

Jenna looked down at her hands, felt another cool breeze blow down Main Street, carrying a few errant dried-up leaves with it.

"It was more than that," she finally said. "I was used to being on my own. Military life prepared me for that. Kent seemed to find reasons to volunteer to be anywhere but where I needed him. So I was alone a lot. And when he died and it was just me and Brian, I realized it was strangely the same as when he was alive and out on a military mission. Being without him wasn't any harder than it had been to be with him. But without a husband tying me to a nomadic life, I realized I really missed Chesterfield. And yes, I missed the quiet and being closer to nature, but what I missed more than anything was the sense of community, the way people band together to help each other. So I came back."

"And have you done that? Asked for help?"

Chuckling, she looked away in embarrassment. "You should know. It seems like the only thing I've been doing with you."

He patted his stomach. "It's not the only thing. Besides, accepting an offer is not asking. You see, when my grandparents came over from Germany after the war, they were met with a lot of anger by Americans who'd lost loved ones overseas. They didn't speak a word of English, but Oma said they didn't need to know English words to understand the anger and unkindness of people who hated them for where they'd come from. So Oma always taught us that kindness came first. It costs you nothing but is worth everything. I try to remember that."

"That's a beautiful lesson."

He shrugged, lifted himself from the bench they were sitting on and threw away his napkin before returning to the bench. "I've taken a lot for granted in my life. I had the illusion of that luxury when I was out on military operations. I guess I've just come not to expect things."

"You talk an awful lot about the military. Not that I mind. Brian loves your stories and so do I.

I'm just curious why you decided to leave when it's clear being a marine was an important part of your life."

Tom's face changed, tightened, and Jenna knew she'd hit a raw spot. She knew those spots hurt plenty. She had her own raw spots, and wondered quietly if she'd just forced open a wound that Tag was having trouble healing.

Wishing she could take back her words, Jenna quickly said, "It's none of my business. You don't have to answer that."

"No, it's okay." Tom thought a moment, and after a brief pause he continued. "Like for all things in life, I decided it was time. Some things just have a normal shelf life, and the military had reached its expiration date for me."

She smiled at his metaphor. "That simple, huh? I guess that's a good way to put it."

He grinned. "I have my moments. There are things I miss about being a marine. But my life has moved on."

He sounded convincing, but Jenna had known plenty of people in the military, and experience had shown her that once a military man, always a military man. If he had the chance, would he run back into active duty? Many military men did.

She wondered just how long it would be before the pull of service would claim Tom. And what she'd do if he left.

Chapter Five

"You were in the military a long time. Do you ever think you'll miss it?"

Jenna's question had Tag thinking about the job offer he'd received from his CO to work at Fort McCoy training Army Rangers.

Miss the military? Maybe. Wolf had suggested as much when he'd urged Tag to take the position. Fort McCoy wasn't too far from where their family lived and Tag knew the whole family would like nothing better than for him to accept the position. But if he did, his days would be filled with memories he just wasn't ready to face. Memories that might cause the return of old problems.

The flashbacks that had plagued him during his recovery when he'd first returned home from Afghanistan had all but ended. He hadn't had a single flashback of his captivity or time in the military since he'd moved to Chesterfield. Life here was too different, with nothing to remind him of things he'd much rather forget. He liked it that way.

No, it was best that he stayed put. Chesterfield was far enough away from his family that he could lick his wounds and start a new life.

It surprised Tag just how much he liked talking with Jenna Atkins. He wasn't a chatty guy by any means. But she had a funny way of getting under his skin, and it didn't feel as uncomfortable as he thought it might.

Chesterfield had just been a dot on the map when he'd purchased the old Nelson farm, but Jenna's friendship had changed that. Now it was starting to feel more like home.

"I was offered a training position at Fort McCoy. But Chesterfield is growing on me."

"Well, I'm certainly glad you moved on to here," Jenna said. "I came back to Chesterfield because I wanted a stronger support network to lean on, but I never could have guessed the way a complete stranger would step in and make my life so much easier."

Her open appreciation made Tag feel a little embarrassed. "You seem like you have it all together. You've done a good job handling your job and Brian."

Jenna shrugged. "That's just it. I've handled it." Deciding she was losing the battle with her melting ice cream cone, she tossed what was left of it in the trash and wiped her hands. "It was only when I came back to Chesterfield that I realized I really needed someplace safe to vent my fears or at least have a good cry every now and then. I can't do that when I'm alone with Brian. He needs me strong."

Tag thought of how many times Nancy had complained about that very same thing. When Crystal was four, she'd had a high fever from the chicken pox she'd gotten from one of the kids at day care. He'd been out on a mission, leaving Nancy to handle it alone. No one could even get in touch with him when Nancy had appendicitis. Crystal ended up staying with one of the other families on base while Nancy healed. Tag hadn't heard anything at all about her surgery until he'd returned.

He hadn't been there for his family, and he was getting a clear picture of how that felt from the other end as he listened to Jenna.

Jenna covered her face with her hands and then

pulled them away, shaking her head. "I've said too much again."

"No, you didn't."

"Yes, I have. I have a tendency to do that. You were just starting to get comfortable, and now I've made you crawl back into that shell you've been hiding in again. I didn't mean to heap too much on you."

"Isn't that what friends do? Talk about their feelings?"

"Some people have an easier time than others. Being the only female in my house leaves me jabbering on, I'm afraid."

"It's okay."

She leaned forward, resting her elbows on her knees. "You remind me a little of those cowboys you see in old Western movies."

He chuckled. "A cowboy? How so?"

Jenna glanced up and thought a bit. "You're the strong, silent type. You walk around like you've got a lot on your mind, but you don't share much. You help take care of others, do what needs to be done, but like those cowboys, you're fine alone. They don't need much and don't ask for anything."

"Not unlike me coming here to Chesterfield? Maybe I need to get a dog and a horse."

Her face was filled with questions, which made Tag want to bolt from the bench.

"And usually they're wounded. Is that what happened to you, Tom?"

He shifted, and Jenna immediately sat back.

"Now I have said too much. I'm sorry."

"It's okay."

"I can't seem to keep my thoughts to myself when I'm around you, and now I've made you uncomfortable again."

She was too close to something he wasn't ready to talk about. He wondered if there'd ever be a time when he'd feel comfortable opening up about what had happened. Today wasn't the day to do it, though. That much he knew.

"If you don't mind, that story is best kept for another time."

"Fair enough," she said quietly, watching the sun sink lower in the horizon. Brian would be coming home soon. "Besides, if I don't get home to put that roast in the oven soon, none of us are going to eat dinner. And then my dad will be a grumpier old man than he is right now."

"Get ready for bed, Brian," Jenna called out from the kitchen. She'd just finished washing the last of the dinner dishes while Tom and Brian played video games in the living room.

Since Tom had planned on coming over for dinner, anyway, it hadn't made sense for her father to pick her up in town. Tom had driven her back to the farm, to Brian's delight when he got home from David's to find Tom already there. Dinner had been filled with conversation about the truck and Brian's playdate with David. He seemed to have had a good time, so Jenna made a mental note to make plans to have David over to the farm next week.

For now, she knew she should be focusing on all the work she had to do tonight after Brian went to bed. And yet, she wasn't ready to cut her evening short by having Tom leave.

"I don't want to get ready for bed," Brian said, dragging himself into the kitchen, Tom walking in behind him.

"You know the rules," said Jenna. "I'll never get you up for school if you don't get to bed on time. Now get upstairs and get ready for your bath."

Brian scurried out of the room, and she heard him stomp his way up the staircase.

From the other room her father called out, "Easy on the feet, Brian!"

Tom smiled in response to the commotion that

was so normal a part of her life. Then he said, "If I make it to Valentine before Brian's next dialysis treatment, I'll exchange the part for the truck. Otherwise, we'll wait until we go together."

"I want you to know I appreciate everything you've done for us, Tom."

He gave her a crooked grin. "Now, if you go thanking me every time I do something, I'll feel like I'm overextending my boundaries."

She cocked her head to one side. "How could you be overextending your boundaries? I'm the one who is getting all the favors."

"I'm not the only one doing favors here, Jenna."

"Friendship is not a favor."

His eyes warmed. "No, it's a gift. Are we friends?"

"I'd like to think we're becoming friends. Even if you do hide yourself behind that wall so much."

He chuckled on a sigh. "Is that what I do?"

"Don't pretend you don't. Except, of course, when you're with Brian. He seems to bring out the kid in you."

He gave her a smirk. "Not everyone is an open book like Brian. He makes it easy."

She laughed quick and loud. "You can say that

again. But I have to admit, it's something I love about him."

"Me, too. He's a great kid."

"Yes, he's a blessing. But he is a handful, and it makes it hard for me to fulfill my orders for Eye for Style."

He raised an eyebrow. "Eye for Style?"

"My company. Clothing designs. I got tired of the kinds of clothes we found on the base or in some of the stores where we were stationed, and I was pretty bored, so I started drawing sketches of things I liked and then sewed them myself. Some of the other women on base liked what I was doing and asked me to sew for them. It grew into a cottage industry. It helps pay the bills."

"Wow. I'm impressed."

"Well, don't be too impressed yet. It's a small company."

She couldn't help but feel flattered by Tom's response.

"Sounds like a win-win situation."

"Definitely. Now that I don't have to worry about rent, I can save money and put it aside for when Brian needs a kidney transplant. And he *will* need one eventually. I'm hoping Brian can ward off a lot of the problems my late husband had by early medical intervention and an eventual transplant. But right now he's not sick enough to even be put on the donor list."

She glanced at Tom, who was hanging on her every word. For now. In her experience, military men got restless. How long would the newness of Chesterfield hold a man like Tom Garrison before he got the itch to leave?

Tag pulled himself toward the kitchen door, away from the concern on Jenna's face. The worry in her eyes over Brian's condition was hard to ignore. He'd seen that same type of alarm in the expressions of his family when he'd first returned from Afghanistan.

His parents, grandparents, even his cousin Wolf, all wondered if what he'd gone through as a POW had been too much for him to take. The flashbacks he'd initially experienced had been severe enough that even he'd had doubts as to whether he'd ever be able to get through the day without reliving the horrors of captivity.

But unlike his family, who always wanted to know what he was thinking and feeling, wanting him to remember things that were too painful for him to deal with, Jenna didn't push any further than Tag was willing to go.

And Tag wasn't ready to go back to his memories

of captivity. No matter what any military shrink said about learning to deal with his memories rather than pushing them away.

His family and his doctors had been dead set against him coming out to Nebraska alone. It was clear they thought it would be better if he stayed back in Wisconsin with his family, kept his feet wet in the military by working at Fort McCoy.

But what he needed was the opposite of what Jenna craved. Tag didn't need to have his living relations hover over him with worry. He needed to start living his life again and learn to function without the weight of memories pulling him down.

"I enjoy your company, Tom," Jenna said as she walked him to his truck. "Brian does, too. And what you're doing for us—"

"I need to go to Valentine for supplies anyway. John Peers has been ordering for some of the other businesses in town, too, so it looks like I'll be kept busy—for a while, anyway. There's no trouble in taking you and Brian along with me."

"Then I'm grateful for it. And the extra time in my day to work."

She drew in a deep breath, but kept her distance. He was glad of that. Jenna was an affectionate woman and had an impulsive way of ending up in his arms, rattling him.

They said their good-nights, and he climbed into his truck. His eyes roamed to the rearview mirror. She was just standing on the porch steps, watching him drive away. He could see her clearly under the porch light.

He wasn't exactly sure if he liked the unsettled feeling it gave him. But there was something stirring inside him that made him want to keep looking in that rearview mirror to see if he could still make out Jenna's image.

With eyes firmly planted on the road ahead, he blew out a quick breath. "Stop lying to yourself, Tag," he grumbled to himself. "So Jenna has pretty eyes. Big deal." And she could talk up a storm even when he had nothing to say.

He was already looking forward to the next time he'd see her again.

Chapter Six

Tag washed the engine grease from his hands using the outside faucet rather than dirtying up Jenna's sink in the kitchen. After inspecting his hands and deciding he'd gotten enough of the grime off, he wiped them dry with a clean rag. Working on an engine wasn't exactly a white-collar job that left your fingernails clean. But it sure was satisfying when he got it up and running again.

Tag hadn't spent a lot of time working on car engines, but he had worked on planes. His love of aircraft didn't stop with flying. An engine was an engine, and he'd managed to figure out a thing or two on Ben's truck that would hopefully make it run farther than up the driveway before conking out on Ben or Jenna.

It surprised him how much he liked all their

company. These last months he'd spent pretty much by himself, not wanting to be around anyone else or have others intrude on his feelings, or ask questions he wasn't ready to answer.

He'd seen those same questions behind Jenna's eyes. But when he'd shut himself down in front of her the other night, she hadn't pried any further. And that made him feel comfortable enough to wonder if he'd been keeping himself hidden away long enough. He could use a little time out of hiding. He'd liked what little venturing into the real world he'd done where Jenna and Brian were concerned.

On his last trip to Valentine he'd exchanged the part for Ben's truck. Between the two of them, Ben and Tag had—with Brian's enthusiastic, if unskilled, help—managed to get the engine running with a smooth purr. There were no guarantees with a vehicle this old, but after a quick drive to test it out, Tag figured the truck would be dependable enough for both Jenna and Ben to use around town. They had some miles left before they had to worry about dumping a load of money on a new vehicle and making high truck payments.

Ben took care of parking the truck after dropping Tag outside the front door. As he walked into the house, Tag heard stomping on the floor and a door upstairs slam.

"Brian!" Jenna hollered.

"No! Go away!"

The muffled voice was probably caused by Brian burying his head in the pillow as he screamed. Brian had been fine during dinner. He'd excitedly gone on about a field trip that was coming up at school. Tag wondered what had happened to bring on this tantrum.

Jenna flew through the screen door and onto the porch. Her nerves seemed as frazzled as the hair coming out of her ponytail.

"What's going on?" Tag asked as he followed her outside.

She closed her eyes and shook her head, lifting a plastic cup filled with liquid in the air. "Tomorrow the doctor is doing a CAT scan on the organs surrounding Brian's kidneys. He needs to drink this barium drink tonight."

Tag made a disgusted face. "Does he really have to?"

Jenna cocked her head to one side. "Be serious. Of course he does."

"Poor little man. That stuff is nasty."

"You've had it before?"

"Unfortunately. Since it's clear he doesn't want to drink it, I take it he's had it before, too?"

Jenna sighed. "Yes. And it was a battle to get him to drink it the last time, as well. But he needs this dose tonight and another one tomorrow, right before the procedure. As stubborn as that boy can be, he'll probably clamp his mouth shut from now until we pull up to the hospital tomorrow. If I can even get him to go. He's flat out refusing because he knows what's coming."

Ben breezed by the porch on his way to the barn and called out, "Stubborn? My grandson? He comes by it honestly. Reminds me a lot of you."

"Very funny, Dad." She tossed him a wry look and rolled her eyes. "You're not making this easy, either. I need you to come help me get Brian to cooperate."

Ben shook his head. "Can't do it. I need to round up those piglets and get them in the pen again. Brian keeps letting them out to play with them and then forgetting to tell me. I just saw one of them running free out toward the field. If it gets into the crops, we'll never find it tonight and it could die."

Propping a hand on her hip, Jenna said, "Ter-rific. Yet another thing I have to talk to Brian about. He can't be letting all the farm animals run free."

A slow smile crept up Tag's face. "Well, the safety of the animals is a serious situation, but I can't say that I blame him for being opposed to drinking that barium drink. Have you tried it? If you put that thing in front of me, I'd go running for the hills."

Her sweet lips pursed, and she started to chuckle. "You're as bad as he is sometimes. This is a serious situation. He has to do this, Tom. It's the only way the doctor can see if his condition is stable."

Tag put up his hands in surrender. "I know, I know. I'm just sympathizing with the little man. You know, as one male to another."

With a piglet in his arms, Ben laughed as he walked around to the other side of the barn.

"Dad?"

Ben didn't looked back as he hollered to her. "Tom can do the honors tonight. Maybe he can talk some sense into the boy. He won't listen to me, either."

Her shoulders slumped as she sighed. "These are the times I wish Kent were here for reinforcement. My father is great, but Brian has him wrapped around his little finger."

"Look, if you want me to talk to him, I will. I'm not sure it will help, but it couldn't hurt."

"If you can convince him to drink this whole cup down, I will be forever grateful." Her face changed. "The warmer months are always worrisome. He has to drink a lot of fluids to help flush out toxins, and if he doesn't—and he doesn't—he could develop an infection. The doctor needs to know if there are any changes in his condition."

She blew out a quick breath that lifted the hairs on her forehead.

Tag took the cup of barium from Jenna's hand. Their fingers brushed for just a moment. As he lifted his eyes to hers, he took the cup and saw tears welling in her blue eyes. It must be hard to have to handle Brian's medical issues and his rambunctious behavior.

"We'll have a talk. I'll see what I can do."

She nodded quickly, holding herself around her middle as if holding herself together. "Thank you. Have him leave the empty cup on the bathroom sink. Not in his room. I don't want to find it in the toy chest or under the bed three weeks from now."

Tag walked away, wondering if that simple touch had sent a shock wave through her as strongly as it had hit him. It had been just a brush of their fingers. Simple human contact. Yet even that small amount had been missing from his life for a long time.

As he climbed the stairs, he tried to remember what it had been like the last time he'd seen Nancy, before he'd been shipped overseas. Sadly, those days were a blur—not because he didn't want to remember them, but because they'd been too few toward the end. It was one of his biggest regrets.

As he reached the top of the stairs, Tag heard Jenna's voice outside through the second-floor window just above the porch. She was relaying her current frustration over Brian as Ben tried to console her.

With determination, he turned toward Brian's bedroom. After a quick knock on the door, he waited, but Brian didn't answer. Pushing the door open, he paused. A child's bedroom held so many things. It was a sanctuary that only those close enough were permitted to enter.

"Brian?"

No answer. Tag walked inside and glanced around the room. The crimson lava lamp on the nightstand came alive with movement. The superhero comforter on the bed was pulled back and rumpled over a pile of Legos that had yet to be put away. Brian wasn't visible in the room, and Tag took a second to think of all the little crevasses that would make a perfect place for a child to explore.

Or hide.

Under the bed was too obvious, and Brian was too creative for that. It would be the first place Jenna would look. The closet was another dead giveaway.

Tag's eyes landed on a large toy cabinet, which sat kitty-corner between two windows. The door was shut and toys that should have filled it were piled high on the floor and on Brian's bed. Figuring he'd hit pay dirt, Tag made his way toward the cabinet, knocking on the white painted wood as he crouched down.

"Can I come in?" he asked.

After a brief pause Brian spoke from behind the cabinet door. "You won't fit."

Tag smiled. "Then I guess you'd better come on out so we can talk."

The cabinet door creaked as it opened to reveal Brian sitting Indian style on the bottom shelf. He was hunched over, clutching a Bionicle and a flashlight, the back of his head pressed up against the shelf above.

"I don't want to."

Tag lifted an eyebrow. "Then you leave me no choice but to join you in there."

Brian was slow in turning, but Tag knew he was home free when the corners of Brian's cheeks pulled back and then he burst into laughter.

"Don't worry. It's safe. Your mom's outside with your grandfather. It'll be just you and me."

As he climbed out of the cabinet, Brian's eyes fixed on the plastic cup Tag was holding and frowned. "I'm not drinking anything from that cup. It's gross! No one can make me do it."

"Well, that's true enough. But let's have a chat, anyway."

"I'm not doing it," Brian said stubbornly. He bounced onto the bed and pushed the comforter aside, pitching a few toys over to the floor with a crash. The noise didn't seem to faze Brian, nor did the mess he'd created as he sat there scowling.

"Your mom is asking you to do this only because it's for your own good."

Brian rolled his eyes and looked at Tag.

"Hey, Scout, I feel your pain. I really do," Tag said, putting up a hand in surrender. "This barium drink is pretty disgusting stuff."

"That's right," Brian said with a stern nod.

"That doesn't mean you don't have to drink it, though."

Brian wilted against the pillow, pushing away toys with his foot in irritation. "How come I have to do it? No one else I know has to."

"Says who?" Tag asked. "Last time I had a physical, I had to do it. It was a direct order from my CO. Now, if I had to do it, what makes you think you're so different?"

Brian considered it for a second. "It's not the same. I betcha I've had to do it way more times than you."

Tag sighed as he sank onto the mattress, carefully picking up toys and rearranging them to make room for himself. "Yeah, you're probably right about that. I've never had to see the doctor every week for anything, and no one is poking and prodding me like they do to you. I feel for you. But you know, there are lots of things I *have* had to do in my life that weren't the greatest. Even though I didn't like it, I still had to do them, anyway. I'll bet there are other things you have to do that you don't enjoy so much."

"Like?"

"Like picking up your toys and putting them away."

"That's nothing."

"How about making your bed?"

"Mom does it for me."

"She does? And that doesn't bother you any?"

Brian folded his arms across his chest in an exaggerated way. "That's what moms are supposed to do."

"Oh, really? I must have missed that one when I was straightening my bunk in the barracks."

"Moms don't go into the marines."

Tag held himself back from laughing. The little guy was going to have an answer for everything Tag threw at him.

"Well, some do. But they don't go to make their sons' beds. They go because they're marines, too."

"Girls can't be marines!"

"Oh, yes, they can. Girls can join any branch of the service they want. And they're good soldiers, too. I've met a whole bunch of them." Taking a second to regroup, he thought about what would matter to Brian. "You know, years ago, when I was in Army Ranger School, we used to have to do these drills in the Okefenokee Swamp—"

"You said you were in the marines, not the army."

"I am—well, was. The Army Rangers aren't just for military personnel in the army. There are soldiers from all the branches of the military who go through special training. And it's a big deal, too. You can't just sign up to be an Army Ranger. Only a certain number of soldiers who are smart and fit enough get invited to train and then only a few of them actually finish."

Being chosen to train as an Army Ranger was considered a privilege. Only two soldiers from his unit had been given the chance to even test to see if they had what it took to go into training. He remembered the pride he'd felt when he'd called Nancy to tell her the news and how the silence on the other end of the line had spoken volumes of her displeasure. All it had meant to her was that she'd be home alone a little while longer.

He glanced at Brian, who finally seemed interested in something other than the drink Tag held in his hand.

"We'd go out into the swamp for a couple of weeks at a time. The team had to survive with just what we had in our packs. Nothing more. If you got your gear wet, it stayed wet until you made it back to your barracks. Sometimes that meant walking around and sleeping in wet clothes and boots for weeks."

Brian's jaw dropped open as he hung on Tag's every word.

"One particular day, while we were hiking through this thick patch of woods, we came to a section of river that we had to cross. Now, like I said, we didn't want to get wet, but we knew we were going to have to if we were going to get across the river. Also, there was no way we could cross the river with the packs on our backs without all our gear getting wet. The water was too deep and the packs were too heavy to hold over our head and maneuver as we walked through the running water."

"What'd you do?"

"We had a choice. We could all go in and get ourselves and our stuff completely wet and end up being miserable about it. Or one of us could strip down and then wade through the water to the other side so we could fashion a rope bridge to pull all our packs across. That way we could keep the gear and our boots dry."

"You got chosen to get wet, didn't you?"

Tag laughed along with Brian. "Well, we were all going to get wet, but I was the one who had to take the first swim. Now, I just knew there were all kinds of creatures, like eels and snakes, living in the swamp."

"Did they bother you?"

"Not the eels and snakes. But they weren't the only things living there."

Brian stared at him wide-eyed, as if Tag was

telling him a horror story. "What was living there?"

"Do you really want to know?"

"Yeah!"

"I managed to get about halfway across when I felt something under my foot. You see, I didn't want my boots to get wet, so I took them off and left them back onshore with my gear. At first, I thought an eel had moved under my foot. At least, I'd hoped it was only an eel. But eels don't feel that solid."

"They're slimy."

"Right. But this thing felt hard, like a rock, only it was moving. Then I hoped maybe I'd stepped on a snapping turtle's shell. I didn't want to mess with one of those, so I decided to move quick. Then I felt a snap just miss my heel."

"Did the snapping turtle bite you?"

"Hold on. I'm not done telling the story. I started to swim faster, because I didn't want anything biting me. I had the rope in my hand and felt another snap, which just missed my foot. That's when I realized whatever was down there was too big and was swimming too fast to be a snapping turtle."

"What was it?"

"An alligator."

Brian jumped to his knees on the bed. "No way! Really? You stepped on an alligator?"

"Right on its head."

"Koowell!"

Tag sputtered, "You wouldn't have thought that if you were there and a big old alligator was snapping at your feet."

Brian laughed.

"Now, we all knew alligators lived in the swamp and there was a good chance we'd encounter a few. There were soldiers lined up along the bank of the river, looking out for just that very thing. But this gator decided to go deep, and that's where he found me."

"Were you scared?"

"Well, yeah. Wouldn't you be?"

Brian giggled. "Yeah, I guess so."

Tag heard a creak in the hallway and guessed Jenna was out there listening to his story, seeing if he was making any progress with Brian. Brian was too preoccupied with the story to notice.

"What did you do, Tom? Did he get you? Did he take a chunk out of your foot?" Brian twisted his hands in eagerness to hear the rest of the story.

"Nah, I just swam faster than I'd ever done before, hoping the gator would find something more interesting to give his attention to. In fact, I swam so fast, the soldier on the bank holding the other end of the line got rope burn on his palms before I made it to the other side of the river."

Brian laughed.

"We built the rope bridge and managed to get all our gear to the other side without getting everything soaked. We changed into dry clothes, and no one got sick or miserable because they had to stay wet. My point is that sometimes we have to do things we don't want to do. But we do them because they're for our own good."

Brian's little face skewed up into a frown. "How is stepping on an alligator's head good for you?"

"It was the training that was good. Stepping on the alligator was just an added bonus. I didn't want to get into that water and get wet any more than any of the other guys did. I certainly didn't want to be the first one to have to make the journey without knowing what was in there. But I knew someone had to do it, for the good of the team.

"You see, just like you need to be disciplined because of the problem you have with your kidney, my unit had to be disciplined. Training taught us to work together to do what needed to be done. We didn't always think it at the time, but looking back, it made us stronger. After a while you don't question things. You just do what you have to do. Everything from jumping into the swamp to rushing to get up in the morning, to getting dressed and in line and then waiting until the CO had eaten his breakfast and was good and ready to start a run." He handed Brian the drink in the plastic cup. "Things like drinking a really disgusting drink before an important test when you go to visit the doctor. Even if you don't want to do it."

Brian looked up at Tag, and with his shoulders sagging, he took the cup in his hands.

"Think of it as alligator duty, Scout," Tag added. "Go forth and fulfill your mission."

"Oh, all right," Brian said with a sigh. With a disgusted look in his face he put the cup to his mouth and then shook his head.

Leaning forward, Tag said, "I find it helps to hold your nose while you drink it. It makes it go down easier."

Brian pinched his nose and gulped down the drink, allowing drops of it to dribble out of his mouth and down his chin.

"Am I done?" Brian finally said, still swallowing and making a face.

"Good job. I'm proud of you," Tag said, smiling his approval. "Now go wash your face and rinse the cup in the sink so your mom doesn't have to do it for you."

Brian slipped out of bed and ran out the bedroom door. Tag heard his quick feet racing down the hall and then the slamming of the bathroom door.

As he turned to get up from Brian's bed, he saw Jenna standing in the doorway. He'd known she was standing there, but she'd kept her distance. The look on her face… If he lived a thousand years, he wouldn't forget that look of gratitude.

"Want to have a cold drink on the porch before you head out?" she asked. "I promise it's a whole lot better than what Brian had to drink."

She was pretty even with fatigue pulling at her eyes. Her hair had become mussed from doing work and was wet on the side of her head, as if she'd tucked a few locks behind her ear while she'd been washing the dishes.

A cold drink on the porch with Jenna sounded good. But he knew that what he really ought to do was go home. He'd become altogether too comfortable here, and that couldn't be good. Besides, it had been a long day, and tomorrow would be even longer if he didn't manage to get some sleep tonight. "I should really get home," he finally said.

Jenna did her best to hide her disappointment,

but he saw it in the slight fading of her smile. "Give me a second to tuck Brian in and I'll walk you out."

As Tag started down the stairs, the toilet flushed and the bathroom door abruptly flew open, banging on the inside wall.

"All set, Scout?" he called up.

"You betcha!" Brian yelled.

"Okay, off to bed with you," Jenna said from the top of the stairs. "I'll be in your room in a minute to tuck you in. Put your toys away!"

"Aw, Mom!"

"Don't 'Aw, Mom' me."

As Tag walked downstairs, the chatter between Jenna and Brian continued. For a moment he was taken back to a time that felt familiar, but it was still too painful to allow himself to linger in the memory.

Ben was sitting in front of the television, watching a game show. Tag could wait for Jenna in the living room while he talked to Ben. There was no need for her to walk him out to the truck. He could easily thank her for dinner and say his goodbyes right now. End it at that.

But he needed a moment, he decided. He wasn't ready to let go of the quiet evening he'd shared with Jenna and her family. He wouldn't allow thoughts from the past to intrude on what little peace he'd been able to capture here, especially since those peaceful moments had seemed too rare over the past year.

He pushed through the screen door and stepped onto Jenna's front porch, not bothering to flick on the light. Instead, he breathed the late spring air deeply and let it out slowly.

As he looked up at the deluge of stars in the dark sky, he was reminded that he was no longer a marine. He was in Chesterfield, Nebraska, not Afghanistan or anywhere else in the world. What happened in the past couldn't hurt him anymore.

If he continued telling himself that, then maybe in time the memories that haunted him every day and night would begin to fade and he'd finally feel peace.

Chapter Seven

Jenna didn't quite know what to make of it. Brian responded to Tom in a way he didn't to her or her father. It didn't really surprise her that Brian manipulated her father. Brian knew how to get his grandfather to roll over, and as hard as her dad tried, he still spoiled his grandson. But Tom's help with Brian was an unexpected gift. Brian idolized the man, making Brian downright eager to follow Tom's requests. And Tom was a perfect authority figure with Brian—patient and understanding, but never giving way as he explained to Brian what the boy needed to do. The only downside was that Jenna was getting too used to leaning on Tom for help and support, and that was a dangerous habit that she'd need to avoid.

She tucked Brian into his bed, giving him a kiss on his cheek. He smelled clean from his bath earlier that night.

Jenna had always enjoyed this special time at night with Brian when it was just her and her son. They said their prayers, and she pulled the blanket over him, tucking the ends neatly under the mattress to make him feel snug.

"Mom?"

"What is it, honey?"

Brian pulled himself out from underneath the blankets she'd just tucked in and sat up. "Do you think he'll come to the festival with us?"

"'He' who?" she asked, knowing full well Brian meant Tom.

"Tom. I told him all about it when he was working on the truck with Grandpa."

"What did he say?"

"He didn't have a chance to say anything. Grandpa interrupted when he dropped this big wrench and it fell on his foot and then he said a word I'm not supposed to say."

Jenna rolled her eyes. "Well, I'm glad you're not repeating it now."

"Do you think he'll come with us?"

"It's still a few days away. Get back under the covers." She retucked the blankets and rumpled Brian's hair. "He might be busy, Brian. Tom has a lot of work. Mr. Nelson was sick for a long time, and the farm needs Tom's attention. I don't want you to get your hopes up if he can't come because he has work to do."

"Will you ask him? Will you?"

The pleading look in Brian's tired eyes was bittersweet.

"I'll ask him. Okay, sweetie? Now, to sleep with you."

She kissed him again, then slipped out of his bedroom, turning off the light.

Her eyes met with her reflection in the mirror as she passed it in the hallway. She took a moment to comb her fingers through her hair. She was exhausted, and it showed in the deep crevasses around her eyes.

Shaking her head, she decided she was being ridiculous.

"You haven't worn makeup on a regular basis or cared what the state of your hair is at eight-thirty in the evening for nearly eight years, Jen," she chided herself as she took the stairs down.

"What was that, honey?" her father called from the living room.

When she reached the bottom landing, she glanced over and saw him slumped in his favorite chair across from the television. It was a familiar scene she recalled from her youth.

"Nothing, Dad. I was just… Do you mind

listening for Brian in case he gets up? I'm just going to be outside for a little while."

He looked at her and smiled. "Take your time, honey. I don't think I'll be much company tonight. Wrestling with that truck wore me out. I'm going to turn in to bed in a few minutes. I've already said so, but thank Tom again for giving me a hand."

"I will. Good night."

She pushed through the screen door and walked out onto the porch. As she glanced at the porch chairs, her heart sank just a fraction. They were empty.

"Over here," Tag said.

She couldn't see him. But as she stepped off the porch and walked into the darkness toward the sound of his voice, he came into view. Her shoes crunched on the ground beneath her feet as she took each step.

Tom was leaning against his truck, staring up at the stars in the sky. Jenna looked up herself. There had to be a billion stars out.

"They're not as bright in the city as they are out here. The sky looks so big out in the country," she said.

"The city lights drown out their splendor. That's one reason I never much cared for the city."

"You must have hated living on base."

"I was away a lot, in places where the stars were a lot like this. What about you?"

"We lived on base. It was easier that way."

He hesitated a moment. "At least you weren't lonely."

She stifled a sigh. "You don't have to be alone to be lonely."

It was more than she'd wanted to reveal about her marriage, so she moved on to what had kept her sane during those years when loneliness and fear weighed her down.

"I kept myself busy. I started Eye for Style while I was still pregnant with Brian." Wrapping her arms around her middle, she said, "You're really good with kids. Brian adores you."

"He's a good kid. He makes it easy."

"He's not always that way with me."

Tom looked at her now. "The dynamics are different between the two of you. I'm not his mother."

She sighed. Watching Tom with Brian tonight had driven home the fact that maybe Brian was missing having a father in his life.

"He has his heart set on you going to the church festival with us in a few days. Will you be going?"

"I didn't even know about it."

"Now that you know, you should consider it. You know Brian. He's relentless. He'll keep asking until you say yes. Have you ever thought of having children someday?" she asked. "Something tells me you'd make a great father."

Jenna could feel Tom staring at her, but his expression was lost in the darkness.

"I need to get going," he said abruptly, his voice quiet.

Squashing her disappointment, Jenna nodded. Why did she always seem to put her foot in her mouth around him? She'd wanted time to spend with Tom for herself, not just to deliver the message from Brian. But it was clear they'd all monopolized his time today beyond his comfort zone. Of course, her big mouth didn't help things any.

She stood next to Tag's truck as he opened the door, not ready to say good-night.

A warm spring breeze lifted her hair and tickled her neck. The night noises seemed to be magnified against the silence between them. The smell of hay and newly turned earth coming from the fields permeated the air.

"My father sends his thanks again for all your

help with the truck. I know he likes the company as well as your expertise."

"No problem." He patted his belly and teased, "I was paid well for my services, just as Brian said when he issued the invitation to dinner."

Jenna quirked a smile. "It'd be great if that's all it took to get work done around here." Shaking her head, she laughed. "I'm never going to live that one down, am I?"

Tom smiled. "Hey, you're an easy target."

Her breath hitched in her throat, and she hoped she could find the right words that wouldn't drive Tom away. "You make things easy, too, Tom."

He hesitated a moment and then took a quick step forward, until he was standing just inches in front of her. Light spilled out of the truck from the open door. As she lifted her head, she saw the features of his face etched in the dark shadows that surrounded them.

Slowly, he lifted his hand to her face and grazed her cheek with his knuckles. Jenna closed her eyes as her head began to swim with his gentle touch. Like the man himself, his movements were deliberate but not rushed. He cupped her cheek as he bent his head, and she lifted her face to him. Their lips brushed against each other, drowning out all noise and movement around them.

She'd imagined many times what it would be like to have Tom kiss her, and the reality more than lived up to the daydreams. When the kiss ended, she was surprisingly disappointed. She liked kissing him, loved the intensification of the feeling of closeness and connection she always felt when they were together.

For the first time since well before her husband had died, she felt her heart stir. But as she placed her hand on his chest, he pulled back unexpectedly.

"My hands are still a little dirty," he said.

She laughed softly. "That's okay. There's plenty of grease on this farm to get me dirty one way or another."

She reached for him again, but he captured her hands and held them between them, taking a slight step back.

"Good night, Jenna," he said.

In that one brief moment he'd been with her. She was sure of it. But now he was running away again. *Lord, what happened to him to make him so closed off?*

In the few seconds it took for him to turn and climb into his truck, Jenna replayed the kiss in her mind. Had she overstepped her bounds with him? No. And she hadn't read his reaction to her wrong, either. He'd been the one to kiss *her*.

Tom slammed the truck door shut. "I'll see you in a few days?"

"Sure," she said.

A few days. That seemed like such a long time.

The engine roared to life, cutting into the night sounds. As he put the truck into gear, Jenna walked back to the porch and turned. It was becoming a habit, watching Tom Garrison speed down her driveway. It was clear to her he was running from something. As she watched the taillights of the truck bounce down the rutted dirt drive and then turn toward his farm, she wondered exactly what he was running from the most.

The sweet smell of Jenna still enveloped his senses, even though Tag was sitting in his truck. He watched the headlights bob as the truck rolled over a pothole the rain had created in the road and was thankful that his was the only vehicle on the road. As distracted as he was, he knew he'd be a danger to other drivers.

He'd kissed her, and it was almost as if he could still feel her lips pressed against his. He spotted his driveway ahead and shifted into a lower gear with a sigh.

In many ways he still felt as if he was married to Nancy. The kiss he'd shared with Jenna should have felt like a betrayal. And yet it hadn't. His late wife existed now only in his memories. He was alone, without the family he'd left behind on missions so many times. Now both Nancy and Crystal were gone for good, and he had to make his life by himself.

But was he really ready to be in a relationship with another woman? Nancy's sad eyes flashed in his mind, as they had so many times. Washington, D.C., was calling him. His CO wanted him to reenlist *when he was ready.* He had so much baggage, so many pieces of unfinished business that he carried with him. Could he pick up here with Jenna and her family when he still hadn't truly laid the past to rest?

Jenna was a special woman. Anyone could see that. But he wasn't the kind of man who could give her the kind of stability she needed. He couldn't make Nancy happy. What made him think he could make Jenna happy?

Tag stopped at the mailbox at the end of his driveway. He didn't need a flashlight to retrieve the stack of letter-sized envelopes that had been deposited there earlier in the day. A sales flyer from the feed store and a bigger envelope from a sweepstakes company, proclaiming he might have won a million dollars, were addressed to Mr. Nelson. Tossing all the mail onto the passenger seat, he put the truck into gear and made his way toward the dark house.

He never left a light on while he was gone, and the house looked harshly lonely with no life breathing inside. It was a stark contrast to what he'd left at Jenna's house. But then, he'd forgotten how much a child could make a home hum with energy. His heart ached now to think about it.

With a heavy sigh, he pushed the truck door open, climbed out and then slammed it. Out in the field the dark was his friend, for as long as it lasted.

He unlocked the kitchen door and flicked on the light. Even before he did, he noticed the red light on his answering machine blinking.

He dropped the mail on the kitchen table and hit the play button. The first call was from his mother, wanting to know how he was doing. The message was short and sweet and ended with a request to call. The second one was from Wolf.

"Hey, Tag. Call me or prepare for the consequences."

A grin tugged at Tag's lips. When they were kids, the consequences usually involved a wrestling match that ended up with a broken knickknack in his grandparents' living room and a stern lecture about horsing around in the house from his grandfather. Wolf wasn't here to break anything, but Tag knew his cousin would come up with *some* way to punish him if he didn't comply.

Although he didn't want to rehash old conversations about how he shouldn't have come to Nebraska, Tag picked up the phone and dialed Wolf's number. Hearing his cousin's voice would be good, even if he didn't want to hear the words he had to say.

"Just for the record, you'd lose," Tag said with a chuckle when Wolf answered after the first ring.

"In your dreams," Wolf said, immediately recognizing Tag's voice. "When have I ever lost a wrestling match to you?"

Tag laughed. "What were you doing? Sitting by the phone?"

"Truthfully? Yeah."

Tag's stomach dropped. "Why? What's going on?"

"Thought I'd give you the heads-up on a few things."

"Such as?"

"Your CO called. Again. The brass are determined to make you put on your dress whites and come to Washington."

"What for?"

Wolf made a noise that made Tag groan. The warning Wolf was giving him was something Tag had feared from the day he came home from Afghanistan. The things he'd done in the military on a mission, good and bad, were part of what he'd done for the United States of America. But the government had a way of wanting to give POWs medals, and it wasn't going to let up on him until he agreed to stand in ceremony.

Even when Tag had been recuperating in the military hospital on base after his rescue, he'd known it was only a matter of time before his CO's paperwork made it to the military committee desk that decided who got what in the way of military honors. He'd hoped his name would be lost in the mix of other, more deserving soldiers, those who'd given up their lives for service to their country, but apparently he'd hoped in vain.

"This award ceremony isn't going to be on base like most of them. They're looking to make some noise with it, and I know how much you hate that. I got my invite, and so did your mom and dad."

"Have fun in D.C."

Wolf groaned. "Look, I'm not going to get in

your face about this. I know how much you hate all this fanfare. But when was the last time you called home?"

Tag couldn't remember. Whenever it was, it had been too long.

"I'm fine."

"Yeah, you say that. But that doesn't stop your mom and dad from worrying. I remember how bad those flashbacks were for you. Your mom still can't talk about them. Have you had any more while you've been in Nebraska?"

No one knew better than his parents and Wolf what Tag's flashbacks were like. They'd been there with him in the beginning, when even Tag couldn't remember them, and then later, when the ones that Tag *could* remember hit him hard. Wolf had even taken leave from his position at Fort McCoy for a time to make sure Tag was going to be okay.

But Tag wasn't sure that he was ever going to be completely okay. How did a person get over a loss like he'd experienced? Still, things *had* gotten better. And despite the concern from everyone in his family, moving to Chesterfield had been a good move.

"Washington," he mumbled. "Now, what do they

want to make us go all the way to Washington, D.C., for?"

"It's a big deal. I know you want to forget about what happened in Afghanistan, but there are a whole lot of people who think it's important to remember it."

"I can't."

Wolf sighed. "I won't push you. I just want you to know that Oma and Opa got an invitation, too. And you know what that means."

"I'll suffer the consequences from Oma if I don't at least call her."

Wolf chuckled. "At the very least. Good luck, buddy."

They said their goodbyes, and Tag hung up the phone.

As if answering his musings, his eyes caught the military seal on one of the envelopes he'd dropped on the kitchen table. His shoulders sagged just a little. Did he really want to see what was in that envelope? He didn't need reminders of what he'd gone through in Afghanistan, and he certainly didn't want to relive what he'd gone through when he'd finally made it home. In many ways, his homecoming had been worse than captivity. It still was.

With a quick thrust he yanked the kitchen chair

out from under the table and sat down. Before he pulled the letter out of the envelope, he rubbed his eyes with his thumb and his forefinger and then resigned himself to the inevitable.

Dear Sergeant Garrison:

It is my honor to inform you that due to your unwavering service in the line of duty you have been chosen to receive the Medal of Honor, to be given to you by the president of the United States at a ceremony in Washington, D.C....

Tag didn't need to read the rest. He'd seen enough of these letters to know the details. Only the part about the president of the United States had come as a surprise.

Most military awards were given at ceremonies on base by the major general. It was considered an honor, and Tag knew the people who'd put his name in for recognition considered it so. But Tag thought differently. He'd survived where others had not. As far as he was concerned, there was nothing to celebrate.

If the ceremony were being held on base, Tag could skip it easily enough. His award would be lost among those of the other soldiers, who were sure to be receiving the same honor. His name would be nothing but a footnote on the paper. But any ceremony warranting the attention of the president of the United States would be given major press, a spotlight Tag didn't want shining on him or his deeds. No matter how many lives had been saved.

No doubt Pike's family would be there, accepting his award for him. Tag's chest squeezed just thinking of his friend who hadn't made it home.

He dropped the letter on the table and rubbed his hand over his face, his mood suddenly changed. Why didn't they just leave him alone? Why was it that every place he turned, someone wanted to make him remember? He didn't need reminders, and he didn't need a medal to acknowledge the deeds he'd done in service to his country. He wanted to be let alone.

A restless energy flowed through his veins as he looked around his house. Where he'd felt life at Jenna's place, he now felt as if his homecoming here had sucked the life out of him, just as it had when he'd returned from Afghanistan.

Lord, when will this ever end?

Moving to Chesterfield had changed that to some degree. Nebraska was far enough away from the memories that haunted him to give him momentary peace. Now he was certain that no place on earth would be far enough to run from the pain of what the United States military wanted to honor him for.

Chapter Eight

Their trips to Valentine had become routine already, measured by the time it took for the flight, the wait while Brian underwent dialysis and then the flight home. Tag normally spent some of his time picking up supplies Mr. Peers or one of the other local businesses had ordered. But he'd already picked up the supplies for Mr. Peers, so he decided to find the little coffee shop near the hospital and spend his time eating a slice of pie and reading the newspaper.

His time with Jenna and Brian had become important. He looked forward to the mornings when the sound of Jenna's truck drew him to the window. He would push back the curtain to see her truck coming down his driveway and his mood would immediately lift.

After the kiss he'd shared with Jenna the other

night, he'd found himself listening for Jenna and Brian this morning with anticipation. The kiss wasn't something he'd planned to do. But he couldn't say he hadn't thought about it before or even since. Jenna had a way of putting a smile on his face even when he was down.

He'd spent the night stretched out on the sofa, staring at the cracks in the ceiling of his old farmhouse. And feeling mighty guilty that he actually liked how Jenna's lips had felt against his when they'd kissed last night. *That* was what was on his mind all night? Not the award, or the mission that triggered it, or Nancy and Crystal?

Had it been so long since he'd kissed a woman that he'd forgotten the way it made him feel? Or was it just Jenna?

He was reluctant to think it was only Jenna that made the storm that normally raged inside him suddenly quiet. He'd come to Chesterfield to get a new start, to stop thinking so much about painful things he couldn't change. He'd wanted to get lost in the physical work of the farm. And he'd hoped that at the end of a long day's work he would be exhausted enough to collapse into dreamless sleep.

He hadn't planned to spend his days thinking about a woman when there was so much work to be done. The fields had been plowed, but from what Ben had told him, Tag was already behind in seeding. If he didn't get moving soon, he'd be lucky if a worthy crop came up at all this year.

As he walked the few blocks to the coffee shop close to the hospital, he thought about how different his life had become from the one he used to live as a marine. Moments of importance had turned from dangerous military missions to simple pleasures like a few hours of flying with Jenna and Brian.

He was crossing Main Street, the newspaper he'd been reading tucked under his arm, when he heard a horn blast from an oncoming bus. Tag snapped his gaze in the direction of the noise, and for a split second he wasn't in Valentine anymore. The street wasn't filled with people shopping and running back to work after a long lunch. He was in Afghanistan. The bus didn't hold people busy with their day. It held children, terrified and screaming.

Tag's heart raced as adrenaline tore through him. He glanced around for Pike. Where was Pike? But the instant he searched, the image faded and he was standing in the middle of the street in Valentine, Nebraska, again. A cab honked loud and long, stopping short in the middle of the street just as the realization hit Tag.

Slowly, he made his way to the curb and took a deep breath as he wiped his forehead with the back of his hand. It had been more than four months since he'd had a flashback, so long that he'd actually forgotten that his post-traumatic stress flashbacks had been frequent when he'd come back from Afghanistan. He'd thought they were over. But his doctor had warned that simple sounds, phrases or smells could be a trigger and he could experience more.

It had to have been the sound of the bus, he decided. Now the noise in his head was unbearable, but he pressed on.

Glancing at his watch, Tag figured he had time enough to have a cup of coffee and get himself together before Brian's session was over. He headed to the coffee shop, where he could see life all around him and forget the deaths in his past.

Tag pushed through the coffee-shop door and found the same booth he'd sat in the last few times he'd gone there. He liked the corner booth by the tinted window, where he could be invisible to the people coming into the coffee shop, but see everything that was going on around him and on the busy street. He'd always chosen his seat well while in Afghanistan. Choosing wrong meant you'd get a little more attention than you wanted from the guards.

Then and now, attention was the last thing he wanted. Peace and quiet were what he'd been craving. He thought Nebraska would give him that.

It had just been a place to hide from old wounds. But apparently the wounds weren't yet willing to let him go.

The waitress immediately came to the table with a half full pot of coffee and an empty cup. Setting the cup down on the table, she said, "Can I tempt you with some fresh pie? We've got blueberry and apple."

"Make it apple pie, heated," he said. "And drop some vanilla ice cream on top."

"Coming right up," she said with a smile.

Grabbing his napkin, he blotted the wet spot on the table where his coffee cup had left a ring.

"Hey, aren't you the guy I just read about in the paper? The marine?"

Tag lifted his head to find two women in their fifties, one holding a copy of the *New York Times,* the other hitting her on the arm and smiling triumphantly.

"I told you it's him. I couldn't believe my sister

and I were just sitting here reading this article about the war hero who's going to be decorated by the president and here you are, sitting right in this little coffee shop in Valentine. A bona fide hero. Rose said it couldn't be you, but—"

"It's not," Tag blurted out, feeling only a twinge of regret for his lie. "I have one of those faces, you know? Everyone is always thinking I'm someone I'm not."

No truer words were ever spoken.

"I told you so," Rose said, rolling her eyes at her sister. "Louise is always hoping to see John Travolta or George Clooney out here in Nebraska. I'll bet you aren't even in the military. Am I right?"

Rose was clearly happy that she'd outwitted her sister. It gave Tag no pleasure to see Louise bested when she was spot-on about identifying him. But he didn't want to talk about what the *New York Times* had written about him, either.

"Have a nice day, ladies," he said as they turned toward the counter. He heard them mumbling as they made their way to the cash register, check in hand.

"He could be a dead ringer for that guy in the paper."

"Maybe it's his brother."

"You never know about these things."

The waitress placed his pie on the table in front of him. His appetite gone, he pushed it aside and watched the ice cream melt on top of the warm pie. He didn't have to read that newspaper to know what it said. It must have included a nice shot of his military picture, too, from what these ladies had to say.

He dropped a ten-dollar bill on the table to cover the tab and a hefty tip and then got to his feet. From the other side of the room, the waitress called out, "Hey, you didn't even touch your pie."

He just waved to the waitress in reply and then pushed through the coffee-shop doors.

The warm spring air hit Tag in the face as he walked out onto the sidewalk. He got to the airport in record time. As he prepped the plane for takeoff and waited for Jenna and Brian to arrive, he fumed. He'd been running from something a long time, trying to get away from the pressure he felt from others who wanted him to remember. But if this afternoon's encounter in the coffee shop was any indication, even a small town in Nebraska wasn't far enough to hide from what he was running from.

"Do you think he'll come? Huh? Huh?"

Brian had chattered on about the festival nonstop since breakfast, on the plane ride to Valentine, through the CAT scan, which had, thankfully, gone well, though the results wouldn't come in for a few days and now on the way to see the doctor. This was the first year he was going to be able to attend the church festival in Chesterfield, something Jenna had always enjoyed as a kid and, apparently, something all the kids at school were talking about.

She almost wished Mrs. Hathaway hadn't mentioned the festival at all when she and Brian had gone down to the grocery store last week to pick up milk and eggs. But even if Mrs. Hathaway hadn't mentioned it, he would have heard about the annual baseball game played at the festival from one of the kids at recess, anyway.

Which was what Brian was nagging her about today. She'd heard him declare that "all the kids are going to play baseball" about twenty times since breakfast, making it clear he wanted to play baseball with them.

She'd forgotten just how much of a big deal the festival was to the people of Chesterfield. Aside from being a major fundraiser for the church, it was a great time to be out with neighbors and townspeople you rarely got to see, given the wide borders of town property in this farming community. It was unlikely you'd have a chat with a neighbor at your mailbox unless someone happened to be driving by when you stopped to pick up your mail.

The people of Chesterfield loved the festival, and they loved their baseball game. Her dad's intervention was the only reason Brian's heart hadn't been broken completely when she told him he couldn't participate in the game. Ben had told Brian he could help change the numbers on the big scoreboard. When that hadn't been enough to lift Brian's spirits, it had been suggested that maybe Tom would do it with him. Since then, the question of whether or not Tom Garrison would go to the festival had been all that had come out of Brian's mouth.

"For the tenth time, I don't know. You already asked him about it on the plane ride here, so he knows about the festival. But I don't want you to be upset if he can't go."

"He'll go. Garrett said that everyone in the whole town always goes. No one stays home. It's a rule. He'd be the only one in Chesterfield who wasn't there if he didn't go."

"Well, I'm sure if Garrett said that, it must be true. But Tom's not from Chesterfield, so he may not be aware of that *rule.*"

Jenna laughed as she took Brian's hand and led him toward the doctor's office that had become so familiar to them over the past months.

"Maybe Dr. Healy will say it's okay for me to play just this once. Can we ask him? Can we? All the kids are playing, and I want to play, too."

"We can ask him, but I don't want you to get your hopes up or be disappointed if he says it's not a good idea."

"Maybe just this once?"

"Maybe. But if he says no, then you're going to have a big job keeping score. That's an important job, and the players will be counting on you."

As they walked down the hallway, Brian was quiet for the first time since he'd heard about the festival.

He finally said in a low voice, "Maybe Tom's going to want to play baseball with everyone else, too. He probably won't want to do something stupid like keep score."

"You never know. Maybe he's one of those guys who likes to keep score instead of getting his clothes dirty stealing second base."

Brian rolled his eyes. "Tom swims with alligators, Mom. He doesn't care about getting dirty."

"Well…just don't assault him with questions

the moment you step into the plane, like you did on the flight here."

Brian kept up a brave face when Dr. Healy told him he thought it best that Brian sit out the baseball game. He thought it was a fine idea for Brian to keep score and make sure he stayed hydrated. It didn't appease her son at all, and it broke her heart to see Brian's disappointment.

Despite her warning to Brian, when they returned to the airport to head home, Brian did indeed flood Tag with a barrage of questions about the festival and whether or not he was going. Tom listened patiently, but it was immediately apparent that something just wasn't right about Tom this afternoon. She hadn't felt any awkwardness with him this morning on the flight to Valentine. Had something happened since then? Or had he just had more time to think about the night before?

She'd kissed him. It wasn't a kiss of gratitude or friendship. This kiss was much different. She'd felt it.

Jenna wanted to believe that he felt something for her, too, that maybe his feelings of friendship were growing. But it had been so long since she'd been interested in a man other than her late husband that it was very likely she was reading his feelings wrong.

Tom had always been a guarded but friendly man, and Jenna knew he valued his privacy. Perhaps they'd pushed it too far. Perhaps she had.

He had never spoken of another woman in his life, but she'd sensed his sadness when the subjects of marriage or children came up. She hadn't asked, of course. Not all men were open about past relationships. And that was okay. She didn't need to know details if she knew how he felt about her.

But the mood he was in when they boarded the plane in Valentine was far different than any she'd ever seen in him, and she had to wonder what the cause was for the change. That, coupled with Brian's disappointment at the doctor's office, made her edgy. She'd worked so hard to take down that wall Tag had carefully constructed around himself. The other night she thought she'd succeeded in demolishing it for good. Now it was back, and she wanted to know why.

The sky always did wonders for his mood, Tag thought as he looked at the powder-puff clouds around them. The encounter with those women in the coffee shop in Valentine had rattled him some, and he knew Jenna sensed something was wrong. But she didn't push. He was glad for that.

Now that he was getting some distance from the city, his mood was lifting.

Brian was sitting in the front seat for a change. After he had hounded Tag endlessly for days—and hounding was something the kid had down pat—Tag had given in and told Brian he could be copilot today. The boy was obviously pleased, and yet Tag sensed a little apprehension in Brian. He was nothing like he'd been during the flight to Valentine, when he had chattered nonstop about the upcoming town festival. Tag wondered if the trip to Valentine hadn't been all that much fun for Brian, either.

"Ever hear of a barrel roll?" Tag asked, hoping to break Brian out of his funk. He gave a quick glance back and caught the warning look on Jenna's face.

"Please tell me I'm not witnessing two mis-chievous boys instead of one child and a man," she said. "The way you're acting, you sound like you're enjoying my unrest."

Tag smiled playfully, which earned him a very stern glance in warning.

"What's a barrel roll?" Brian asked, his voice filled with excitement.

"Something Mommy doesn't want to experience," Tag quietly told Brian. "Something tells me your mom has a weak stomach."

"Never mind," Jenna said.

"It's when the pilot rolls the plane completely around," Tag explained.

"Cool!"

"No, not cool!" Jenna protested.

"You're looking a little green back there, Jenna," Tag teased.

She gave him a pointed glare. "You behave."

"Can we do one, Tom? Can we?" asked Brian.

"Well, we could try one." Tag turned the yoke just slightly to make the plane rock to one side and then back, but he didn't do a roll. Tag laughed but caught the way Jenna grabbed the seat and stiffened.

"Tom!" Jenna screamed, closing her eyes.

Brian laughed hysterically. "Come on, Mom!"

"Yeah, come on, Mom," Tag prodded.

"You're no fun," Brian said, pouting. To Tag, he said, "Do it again!"

Tag shook his head. "Nah. It's no fun if your mom throws up. Then I'll have to clean the plane, and it'll smell for a week."

Brian made a disgusted face. "You'd have to clean it up?"

"Sure. It's my plane," Tag replied. "Who else is going to do it?"

Brian shrugged. "But it would be her throw up."

Jenna chuckled, rolling her eyes. "Sounds like a good reason not to do a barrel roll, huh, Tom?"

Tag couldn't help but laugh.

"I'm so happy you're both having fun at my expense," Jenna added.

"You make it easy, Jenna."

"Glad to oblige. Just keep the plane nice and steady, will you?"

Tag lifted the plane higher so the land below was lost to them in the clouds.

"Cool. Can we go higher, Tom?"

It was a good thing Brian was belted in his seat, because every time Tag looked over, he looked like he was about to jump out of it.

"I think we can manage a bit more altitude," he said. "How high do you want to go?"

"Much higher. Through the clouds," said Brian. "Can we sit on the clouds?"

Tag pulled the yoke to gain altitude. He wouldn't take them too much higher, but seeing the excitement in Brian brought out the playful nature in him and did wonders to elevate his mood. And he loved hearing Jenna's voice as she protested.

"Higher! I want to go higher!" Brian exclaimed.

The plane lifted, but Tag felt sweat bubble up on his forehead as the words triggered another memory.

Higher, Daddy. I want to go higher.

The little voice in his head replaced everything that was happening in the cockpit. *I want to fly through the clouds so we can kiss the angels!*

His heart was beating rapidly, and his hands white-knuckled the yoke and started to tremble. Tag blinked, trying to focus on the here and now, desperately fighting the images flooding his mind.

It was like a slide show. Each face assaulted him one by one with no letup.

Breathe evenly, he commanded himself silently. He'd done this before, fought the gripping panic and won. He took a deep breath and then another. Brian was sitting next to him. Not Crystal. Brian was there, giggling and oblivious to what had just happened.

Higher. I want to go higher.

They were just words spoken from a child's mouth, Tag reminded himself. But these words Brian had spoken mirrored the words he'd heard Crystal say so many times that it was hard for Tag to push away the flood of memories that came with them and the pain that suddenly gripped his heart.

He looked back in the mirror and saw Jenna's concerned face. But she knew nothing of his flashbacks. And now he'd had two in one day. He'd foolishly thought they were gone for good. *Oh, Jenna, I'm so sorry.*

This was never going to happen again. He'd make sure of it. He needed to call Wolf. If there was one person who would understand what he was feeling, it would be him. He'd talk him down from the ledge, like he had many times over the past year. Wolf would want to talk about D.C. again. But he'd wait. No one understood him like Wolf.

Chapter Nine

"So are you coming, Tom?"

Jenna cringed as Brian jumped up in the seat and practically put himself in Tom's face. He'd asked the same question about Tom going to the festival several times, both on the ride to Valentine and now back. Each time Tom had answered patiently and said he'd think about it. This time he didn't answer at all. But knowing her son, anything short of an affirmative yes wouldn't do.

"Brian, sit down and get that seat belt on until the plane stops," Tom said firmly.

Brian's face dropped at the tone of Tom's voice. "You're not going, are you?"

"I didn't say that."

"But you won't say yes. That's the same thing. Mom does that all the time when the answer is no but she doesn't want to tell me."

Jenna's cheeks flamed. "Brian. Tom is a busy man. He's being very nice about taking us to Valentine. I'm sure that if he can't go, it's for a really good reason, and you need to respect that. Let's leave him alone about this, okay?"

The plane stopped, and Brian sat for a few seconds in the seat, as if he was waiting for Tom to give in and say yes.

"Come on, Brian. Mr. Peers is already here, and Tom needs to help him unload his boxes. And we have to get you back home and do your homework."

"No!"

"Brian." Jenna kept her voice even but firm. "We need to get going so Tom can get back to work."

Brian shook his head. "I'm not moving until he says yes!"

"Listen to your mother, Brian." Tom was standing outside the plane now. The firm tone of his voice was enough to startle Brian.

"Aren't you going to have dinner with us again?" Brian asked.

Jenna's heart pulled at the quiver of Brian's bottom lip.

Tom glanced at Brian and then at Jenna before looking away. "No, I can't. I won't be able to go tomorrow, either. I'm sorry."

"But you said—"

"I never said that I would go," Tom interrupted.

"But who's going to help me keep score? I don't want to do it all by myself," Brian protested.

"I can't. I'm sorry." Tom lifted his eyes quickly to Jenna, the same distant mood he was in earlier showing on his face. "Why don't you just take him home?"

She watched as Tom stalked away, running his hand over his head. She heard him mumble a few words to Mr. Peers as his truck pulled out toward the airstrip, but then he continued on to the house. A few minutes later Mr. Peers turned the truck around and headed back to town.

If not for the bright sunshine above and the warm temperature, she'd be shivering from the chill she'd just received. It wasn't like Tom not to walk them to the truck and say goodbye. Or to be so short with Brian.

"Come on, Brian." She reached out to take Brian's hand and caught the tears rolling down his cheek.

"I hate him," Brian said softly.

Her heart squeezed. "I'm sure he's just really busy. Remember, he doesn't have anyone here to help him do all his work like Grandpa has us. Tom has to do it all himself."

But Brian wasn't listening. He just ran to the truck, climbed in and slammed the door.

It killed Jenna that Brian's mood didn't pick up at all during the short ride back to the farm. Or that he managed to hole up in his room with the door shut for most of the evening before he was ready for bed.

"He doesn't like me very much," Brian said as she tucked him in.

"Who?"

"Tom."

Shocked that Brian had gone to such extremes, Jenna tried to comfort him. "What are you talking about? Tom likes you a whole lot. How can anyone not like a funny little kid like you?" She tried to tickle his belly, but Brian abruptly pushed her hands away.

"If he liked me, he'd go to the festival."

"You can't put conditions on someone's affection, Brian. That's not fair. Tom has a lot of responsibilities. I'm sure he'd love to go to the festival, but he has work."

"You and Grandpa have work, but you're going."

She sighed. Brian was right about one thing. She

had a boatload of work to do herself. She'd bitten off more than she could chew regarding orders. It put a lot of pressure on her to get all the work done. But while skipping many fun activities for Brian's treatments was a fact of life and allowed no room for compromise, she was determined to see to it that he had a chance to be a kid and have fun, even if it meant pushing things aside to make time for work.

No, they had to go, even if it meant she had to be up all night for the next two weeks straight to get her work done.

"Everyone is different," she finally said, not knowing what could possibly take away Brian's disappointment.

"Dr. Healy told me I couldn't play baseball. What am I supposed to do when the other kids are playing?"

She pasted on a smile. "Keep score! You know your grandpa is dying to have your company during the game. Normally he does it all by himself. Just think about how much fun that will be."

He pushed at his blanket with his foot. "I don't want to keep score."

Without Tom. Jenna knew that was what he really meant.

* * *

As the night wore on, the hum of her sewing machine felt like a drill in her head, magnifying the anger building inside of her. It hadn't taken long for her anger to get the best of her, and against her better reasoning, she abandoned her work, climbed into the truck and headed over to Tom's farm.

Jenna white-knuckled the steering wheel, hoping she could rein in her temper when she met him face-to-face. She fought to erase the pained look on Brian's face that continued to invade her mind, but it was no use.

She'd made mistakes in her life. She'd need more than her two hands to count them all, but they were her mistakes and she'd paid the consequences for them. Brian was innocent. If kissing Tom had freaked him out, then that was fine. He didn't have to have a relationship with her. But that was no reason to take the awkwardness of that kiss out on Brian.

Tom had to know Brian adored him. She might as well start calling Brian Tom's shadow for the way he'd been hanging on the man for the past few weeks.

Renewed anger of another kind surged through

her, followed by a bitter pain that she couldn't take away, much less change. Brian was starved for a father's attention. And Tom, while not his father, played the role better than Jenna had dreamed any man could. Tom had highlighted how badly Brian needed someone to fill that role, but Brian would suffer even more now if Tom truly was backing away.

Tom was a grown man. If he had an issue with her, then it should stay with her. He didn't have any right to brush off Brian the way he had this afternoon, hurting his feelings. Even with how relentless Brian had been, pestering Tom about the festival, the memory of his tears told her there was no justification for Tom's coldness toward them.

She turned the steering wheel, and the truck cornered the Garrison driveway. As she pulled up front, she saw a dim light from the living room filtering out onto the empty porch.

She knocked on the door a few times and waited for an answer, but got none. Fury grew by leaps, and after she knocked again, she decided she wasn't wasting any more time waiting for an answer. Her hand connected with the doorknob before she could stop herself, and she twisted it open.

"Nice. He keeps the door unlocked at night," she said with a roll of her eyes. "These military men think they're invincible."

She pushed the door open easily and walked into the foyer.

"Tom? The door was open!" she called out. "Tom?"

She found Tom in the living room, in the center of the sofa with the coffee table pulled close. On top of the table, beside some picture frames and a bottle of water was an open photo album, and piles of loose pictures were spread out around him. The TV was on, and the sound of a small child laughing filled the room.

He didn't look up at Jenna as she entered the room. He simply stared at the young blond girl on the television who was calling out to her parents.

"The door was open," she said, feeling some of the fury that had her charging over to Tom's house dissolve.

"I'm sorry," he said. It was a quiet voice. There was no bitterness or anger laced in the simple words. If she didn't know better, she'd think it was defeat.

She lifted her chin. "I came over here because…" A tear trickled down his cheek, and her heart clenched. She glanced at the coffee table, then at the television screen, and listened to the voices of the people talking and laughing. And then she recognized it. Tom's voice. And the picture started coming into view.

Oh, Lord, what have I walked into? Part of her didn't want to know. Yet part of her needed to know what was going on.

She took a cautious step into the room.

"Have you ever been in the abyss, Jenn?" he said, lifting his eyes to her for the first time. There were tears filling his eyes. He moved his jaw and drew in a slow breath as if he was trying to hold them back.

"Abyss?"

"Yeah, you know, that place you go when the pain is so strong from remembering?"

She swallowed. She did know. But this wasn't about her tonight. It wasn't about them. There was something that had Tom by the throat tonight, and it was strangling the life out of him.

Jenna knew she shouldn't have come, but instead of turning away, she found herself drawn deeper into the room by the pleading look on his face.

"What is so painful for you to remember, Tom?"

"You and Brian. You remind me of what I lost.

Every time I'm with you, it's like a gift, and then when I come home, I feel so empty."

Her throat constricted with emotion, and she found it hard to find words. The little girl on the television laughed as the wind blew her hair into her face, and then she pleaded with the man with Tom's voice not to stop the merry-go-round.

"Then maybe it's better if we don't see each other anymore." As soon as the words escaped her lips, she felt a pain deep in her gut and she wanted to take them back. But if she and Brian were truly causing Tom pain, how could they continue?

"Are you sure about that, Jenna?"

"I care a great deal about you, Tom. In the short time we've known each other…"

"We've become close," he said, finishing for her when she fought to find words that would really express what she felt. And then he looked at her, and the room seemed to spin and widen and come alive with just that one look. "I like that. But it hurts."

His eyes turned to the television as the little girl with long blond curls held on tight to the playground merry-go-round and called to her father to push again.

"That's Crystal," he said, his voice breaking.

Jenna turned and glanced at the television screen. "She's beautiful. Who is she?"

"She was my daughter."

Chapter Ten

A cold chill crept through Jenna's veins. The past tense Tom had used when he spoke of Crystal didn't escape her, and suddenly the scene laid out before her took on a tragic clarity.

Jenna didn't want to ask about Crystal. Not because she didn't want to know about her, but because every fear she'd had since Brian was born was sure to be found in what Tom would answer. And yet she did, anyway—not for her, but for him.

Please, Lord, help me be strong enough to handle this right. Help me be Tom's friend and not allow my own fears to make me run from him.

"Tell me about her," Jenna said cautiously. She wanted to put her arms around him and help him let go of whatever pain was gripping him, but she kept her distance in case Tom wanted it that way.

Her anger now banished, she walked into the center of the room and sat down on the end chair opposite Tom. She waited as he brushed a hand over his face and looked up at the ceiling.

"She was killed. It's been nearly two years now, but to me…"

It was like yesterday. She thought the words, knew that was exactly what Tom was about to say and couldn't. If it were her…

Does the pain of losing a child ever go away? Jenna didn't want to ever find out. It had been a nightmare ever since Brian had been diagnosed with his illness as a baby, and yet God had spared her the pain Tom felt right now. But every day the possibility that she would be sitting right where he was seemed all too real to her.

She shook her head to clear her thoughts. This wasn't about her and Brian. Someone had died. Someone Tom had loved dearly. His precious daughter.

Tom's eyes glassed over as he looked at the beautiful girl on the television, laughing as she was being pushed on the merry-go-round at the park.

"When you're in the military, they send you away to some foreign place where you get to be a hero. You fight in a land that is harsh with conditions you wouldn't want your worst enemy to live in. All the time you're there, you're thinking, 'Hey, thank God my family isn't here. Thank God, they're safe in the good ole United States of America.'"

He sighed, dropping his hands from the picture frame, letting it fall to his lap. Another tear trickled down his cheek as he reached for the bottled water on the table and took a quick drink, then picked up a framed picture of Crystal.

He took a deep breath. "And then you come home and find out all the time you were wishing you could hold them, they were already dead, killed in a car accident."

"Oh, Tom. I'm so sorry." She lifted herself out of the chair and started toward him. But he was waving her off, looking away. He wanted distance. She'd give it to him. She stood there and looked down at the coffee table and knew he had spent months living her worst nightmare.

"Today when Brian was sitting in the front seat of the plane, it reminded me so much of Crystal. When she was younger, I'd take her flying and she always said she wanted to fly through the clouds to heaven. Suddenly, that's where I was again, and it hurt so bad that I just wanted to shut it all down and not feel it."

He swiped the wetness from his cheek before going on. "The abyss is good sometimes. Not all the time, mind you. You'd be dead inside soon enough yourself if you let yourself go there too often. But sometimes it helps. And sometimes it even lets you forget the rank stench of the prison with dirt floors and damp, cracked walls that let the sewage from the city seep in. It lets you forget how you lay on a cold, bare mattress with no blanket and shivered until you thought your teeth were going to crack from chattering, wondering if you were going to be a prisoner of war for the rest of your life."

He put the picture of Crystal down on the table and picked up another. "These pictures got me through that. Every time I heard the guards talking about death and slaughter, laughing about what kind of sick games they'd play on us again, all I thought about was this face, this smile and how I'd give anything to come home to her again.

"Every night I prayed until I was sure God Himself was standing in that hole of a prison with me. I bargained with the Lord that if I made it through that nightmare in Afghanistan, I was going to go home and make things right with Nancy. I'd hold my child in my arms and not have to look at the tears in her eyes when I had to leave again. I'd finally hold my wife and find out if there was anything left between us worth saving. And if there was, then I was going to do everything in my power to make it work."

Jenna's eyes filled with unshed tears. She wanted to cry for him, wanted to hold him, but she knew there was nothing she could do to lessen his loss.

She looked at the strewn-about pictures on the coffee table until her eyes landed on a newspaper. It was folded but still revealed the news that the president was going to bestow the Medal of Honor on several soldiers, including one who'd been imprisoned after saving the lives of children targeted by rebel forces. She remembered reading about the soldier's heroics and his return to the United States nearly a year ago. She'd felt such sympathy for the man for all he'd gone through, only to lose his family while he was…

She saw the picture of the soldier wearing his dress whites on the page of the newspaper, and that suddenly enabled her to put it all together. The letter from the Department of Defense she'd seen on his kitchen table the first time they'd had dinner together now took on a whole new meaning.

She didn't mean to gasp, but she did. And when

Tom's face lifted, Jenna saw the recognition in his eyes that she knew.

"This is you?" she asked.

"You heard." He nodded and shrugged, not waiting for an answer. "Of course you heard. It was in the papers at the time, and I'm sure CNN was all over it, from the rescue of those children to my escape against all odds." His voice was bitter. "I'm sure they even had a nice little commentary about what a tragedy it was for me to come home to a dead family."

Everything he said was true and more. His story had dominated the news for weeks, until another tragic event happened overseas that caught the media's attention.

"I don't remember all the details of what happened, but I do know you and your team saved those children before your own capture," she said, crouching down so they'd be eye to eye. She got on her knees and reached for the hand that was holding the picture of Crystal. And Tom let her.

His gaze lifted to her. "I couldn't save my own child. I wasn't here to keep her safe."

"Even if you were home, it might have happened. People get into car accidents all the time. Even the most simple tasks can end up being tragic.

You can't control it. Don't do this to yourself. The what-ifs will drive you mad if you let them."

"They were going to the base because they'd heard I'd been captured. I can't even imagine what my wife, Nancy, was feeling when she heard. It had always been her biggest fear. She blamed me for taking off and playing the hero again when I reenlisted. I deserved her anger. And Crystal… If I'd never gone. If I'd listened to Nancy's argument just once."

"You were doing what you thought was right. You were a marine and an Army Ranger. You wanted to help people, and Afghanistan was where they needed help. She had to have known that. All the military wives and husbands who are left behind know this. We accept it as part of our lives."

He shook his head, clearly not willing to let himself off the hook so easily. "I didn't have to keep reenlisting. In fact, Nancy had begged me not to. I could have put my family first. But I didn't. I loved the military. It was my career. And my family died without me because of it. And now the people who I chose to follow want to give me a medal for abandoning my family."

He lowered his head so his eyes were out of her view, and his shoulders began to shake. His sobs were soft at first and then grew. She went to him, wrapped her arms around his shoulders and just let him cry. There were nights she wished for someone to just hold her like this until her fears faded.

After a few moments Tom pulled away, looking disgusted with himself. "Some hero, huh?"

"Even heroes cry sometimes, Tom."

"Why did you come here?" he asked, his eyes red rimmed and swollen.

Her reasons for coming seemed mighty insignificant now. But he was looking at her, probing her. She wouldn't lie to him.

"I thought you were angry with me."

"Angry? What for?"

She shrugged, embarrassed for even thinking the way she had. "Because of what happened between us. We kissed and…I was confused. You were fine this morning and I thought everything was okay and then you were different when it was time to fly home. You were so distant, and then you snapped at Brian. He was upset and…"

"I'm sorry. I wasn't angry at you or at Brian. I was angry at myself. I didn't want to think about Nancy and Crystal. It hurts too much. But the more time I spend with you, the more I remember and the more I feel guilty for feeling what I do."

"I shouldn't have kissed you last night. If I'd known…"

His eyes widened in challenge. "You wouldn't have done it? That's just it. I would have. In fact, if my memory is correct, *I* kissed *you*."

His admission surprised her more than she wanted to admit, even to herself.

"That's what I mean," he said, reading the expression on her face. "You don't need someone like me, Jenna. Things have a way of becoming way too complicated around me, and you don't need that."

It went both ways. Her life was complicated enough already. That didn't mean they couldn't help each other.

"I do need your friendship. That much I know. It's meant the world to me, even though it's only been a short time. But if you don't want to be a part of our lives, I'll understand."

"I don't know what I want. I just know I don't want to think about it. It hurts too much."

"You loved your family very much. And on some level, it will probably hurt for the rest of your life. I know. Even though things weren't the greatest with Kent, I still feel the pain of losing him when I look at his picture."

Jenna handed him a picture of Crystal and

Nancy. "You can't escape it. And the people you love don't belong in a box somewhere, locked away, Tom. Missing them doesn't mean you have to shut them away from your memory. You don't have to forget them or feel guilty because you lived and they died."

"What am I supposed to do?"

"Celebrate their lives. I'm sure Nancy would have wanted you to move on."

He glanced at the newspaper on the coffee table. "How can I move on if every time I turn around, something or someone wants to make me remember?"

"You need to stop blaming yourself. Nancy wouldn't want that."

"Maybe she would. You would, too."

"No."

"I see it in the way you talk about Kent. I hear it in the things you won't say. You're still angry with him for not being here for you. Truth of it is, I was no different. I let my family down just as much as Kent did."

"Maybe so, but while you may regret not being there for them you can't bear the guilt for their deaths. You didn't take their lives, Tom. Only God has that power."

"Every moment I was locked up in that forsaken

prison, I thought of them. I thought of every time Nancy had stayed awake all night alone while Crystal had a fever. I thought of the resentment on her face when I would leave on a mission and couldn't tell her anything about where I was going or when I'd be home."

Jenna swallowed and paused just long enough to keep the bitterness from her voice. "Military life has a way of doing that to some marriages. She knew what she was getting into when you married. She knew what military life was like."

"That didn't make it easier. Not for her, then. Or for me, now. I wasn't there. I'd made a promise to God. But He gave me heartache instead."

Jenna touched his arm to comfort him and felt him flinch. Did he not think he was worthy of love? Did he really believe God was punishing him for not being there for his family?

"You can't guess what is in God's plan any more than I can answer why Brian was born with a potentially deadly disease." Keeping her distance, she leaned back on the sofa beside Tom. "I wonder ever day why, but I know I'll never get the answers. It's not for us to know why our loved ones have been taken from us. Why they get sick or why we must endure heartache sometimes. We just have to have faith and offer up to God whatever burdens we can't handle."

"Is that what you do when Brian is sick?"

"I try. I'll be honest, it doesn't always work. You've seen for yourself how much I fall short of holding myself together. But I remind myself that every day with him is a blessing, and that all I can do is take care of him as best I can."

She bit her bottom lip, thinking of the tears in Brian's eyes earlier tonight. The same tears that had sent her into a mad fury and had had her racing over here tonight.

She went on. "Tomorrow is the church festival, and from the way he went on about it today, I'm sure you know that Brian wants so badly to play ball and run with the kids. But the danger of him getting dehydrated from overexerting himself in this heat is too great. It breaks my heart my baby can't just be a normal child like all the others."

"He's alive. You can still hold him and love him."

She hadn't meant to minimize his loss by comparing Brian to Crystal. "Yes, I can. And I'll take that for as long as God allows. Even the days like today, when he's difficult to deal with."

Tom drew in a slow breath. "I'll talk to him. I shouldn't have snapped at Brian the way I did."

She looked down at her hands; her irritation at this afternoon's exchange was completely gone. None of it mattered now.

"He can be relentless sometimes."

"It wasn't anything he did. The combination of getting recognized in Valentine, the memories of Crystal on the plane and then feeling uncomfortable with my own feelings made me snap. That wasn't fair to either one of you."

"Someone recognized you? From what? The newspaper?"

"Apparently. The awards ceremony is in three weeks. My CO is trying his best to get me there."

"It's quite an honor."

"It's a medal."

"You don't want to go?"

"Heroes get medals. I'm not a hero, Jenna."

"If you're not a hero, I don't know who is."

His face pulled with fatigue, and she decided not to push him anymore tonight. She reached up and brushed the sweated-matted hair on his forehead away from his eyes.

"You can talk to Brian whenever you'd like. Just drop by the house. If you don't want to bring us to Valentine on Monday, I'll understand. I don't want our time together to be something you dread."

He sighed and leaned back on the sofa.

"Why don't you go to bed? You'll sleep better there than on this sofa."

"I hate that bed. Not just because it's big and empty. It's…lumpy."

She chuckled. "Maybe it's time to get a new mattress the next time you go to Valentine."

He smiled then and started to stretch out on the sofa, his feet slipping behind her. As she moved to stand, he caught her arm.

"Stay for a bit. I won't fall asleep for quite a while. I like it when you're with me. It…quiets me."

She couldn't deny the burst of pleasure she felt at his request. But was Tom really reaching for her? Or was he reaching for comfort out of the pain of losing another woman? She didn't want to be jealous. It had no place here. What Tom needed tonight was a friend and nothing more. But was she wrong to hope for a future with this man that went beyond friendship?

She sighed as she patted his hand.

"I know you can't stay," he said. "I just want you to stay for a little while. I can't sleep, and being alone will just make my thoughts go where I don't want them to go. My dreams are so…"

Closing her eyes, she conceded. How could she

leave him in the state he was in? And deep down, she didn't really want to. He was exhausted. That much was clear. And if he needed her help to rest, then that was what he'd get.

"Okay, I'll stay until you fall asleep."

"Jenna?"

"What?" she said as she slipped her arm around his waist. *To give him comfort,* she told herself. And she was taking that comfort for herself as well, she realized. He'd said she quieted him. She suddenly realized that was how she was feeling about him. There was no doubt she was attracted to him. But there was a quiet calm inside her whenever she was with Tom. She'd never felt that way before.

"How can you look at me and not hate me for being what he was?"

"You're a different man, Tom. We all have choices. Marriages break down for a lot of reasons. I'm convinced I was just as much a part of my marriage falling apart as Kent was."

That admission was a long time coming and it startled her as the words escaped her mouth. She'd come here in anger. She'd found heartbreak and pain when she looked at Tom. And in reaching out to him, she'd received clarity she didn't know she'd been looking for herself.

With a slow sigh, she listened as the room fell silent and the sounds outside filtered in through the open window. A wolf called out from the distant night. Her eyes were drawn to the direction the howls were coming from.

She continued. "A cruel fate took your family before you had the chance to make things right. Only God knows if you and your wife would have been able to work things out. But you can't compare yourself to Kent. You were willing to try. That's all anyone can ask for."

As she sat there in the quiet, she prayed—for Tom, for herself, for Brian. And she thanked the Lord for opening her eyes to some painful truths she hadn't been willing to see before tonight.

It didn't take long for Tom's breathing to become rhythmic. Jenna watched the rise and fall of his chest and the slight movement of his eyes as he fell into a deep sleep. She stayed a few minutes longer just to make sure he wouldn't rouse when she got up.

After turning off the light and the television, she stepped quietly toward the front door, being careful not to knock into anything and wake Tom up again.

As she stepped out onto the porch and made sure the door was securely closed behind her, she remembered how peace had come over Tom's face as he slept. She wondered if she'd be able to capture that same peace after the night they'd shared.

One thing was for certain. Tom had come to Chesterfield to escape the pain of loss. What was less clear was what he'd do when his emotional wounds had healed. There was a very real possibility that he would become restless, just like Kent had. He had a job offer in the military, which he loved. Or maybe he would return to Wisconsin and the family that he loved. How long would it take for the pull of the military or his family to make him leave?

And the very thought of Tom leaving suddenly made Jenna as restless as that wolf crying in the distance.

Chapter Eleven

The sun was scorching, commanding the clear blue sky all by itself. The morning weather report charted unusually high temperatures for this time of year. They really couldn't have asked for a better day for the church festival. All the planning, all the hard work of preparing for this one day was paying off with a record crowd.

Still, a small cloud or two in the sky or a big fat oak tree in the field would be nice, Jenna thought wishfully. She was going to have to watch Brian like a hawk to make sure he stayed hydrated as Dr. Healy suggested. She only hoped that her father didn't get so caught up in the excitement that he forgot to make sure Brian drank plenty of fluids while she worked her shift.

Jenna was scheduled to work the cotton-candy stand for two hours and then relieve Brenda, an old friend from high school, at the barn where the rummage sale was being held. She'd be there only an hour, and then she was free to watch the baseball game with Brian and her father. She wanted to make sure she was there for Brian when the other kids joined in to play.

Her eyes grazed the crowd. She knew she'd been searching for Tom, and yet she didn't know why. After last night's admission, why would he come here today?

You remind me of what I lost.

Jenna didn't know how to take that. The pained look on Tom's face as he gazed at the picture of his late wife and daughter had been heartbreaking. She'd felt an ache in her heart that she didn't want to acknowledge.

Lord, please give me the strength not to be jealous. There's no place for that here.

Jenna had been an air force wife, and she wasn't ignorant to the ways of war. She'd heard the terrifying stories from other spouses about the kind of things that could happen when a soldier was captured. Jenna could only imagine the horrors Tom had gone through in captivity. Despite their problems, Tom had to have loved his wife deeply for that love and the love of his daughter to keep him going during his time of captivity.

To have a love that strong was something she'd hoped for when she'd taken her vows with Kent. That hope had been shattered when their marriage fell apart under the weight of Brian's illness. There'd never been a time to repair that damage before Kent's death. She now wondered if anything would have changed had Kent lived.

Although she'd felt the pain firsthand of losing a spouse, she hoped and prayed she'd never know the pain Tom had experienced in losing a child.

She'd battled her own fear of that fate from the moment she learned her son's health was grave. How could God place this beautiful child in her arms, only for her to live in fear of losing him every single day? And how could she pray for the miracle of a kidney donor when she knew that meant another mother would be suffering the pain she didn't want to feel? The same pain Tom lived with every day.

He'd said that she and Brian reminded him of what he'd lost. Tom was a reminder of the pain she might one day feel, and it terrified her. But Jenna still found herself searching for Tom in the crowd. In spite of everything, she wanted him in her life—and hoped that he wanted her and Brian in his. He had a way of making her laugh and not take herself so seriously. She needed that. She also needed the sense of security he brought, the knowledge that he could and would offer her the support she craved.

"Can I have two?" asked a little brown-haired girl whom Jenna recognized from Brian's class.

"Two? Are you going to have room enough to eat both of these?" Jenna teased.

The little girl giggled. Jenna couldn't remember her name, but she remembered her laughter and those bright eyes that looked so familiar from when Jenna had first visited the school when she enrolled Brian in classes.

"No, silly. I'm going to share one of them with my daddy."

Jenna reached over and handed the girl two cotton candies just as the girl's father came up behind her. She had her father's eyes and smile, but not his blond hair, and she immediately realized why the girl looked so familiar. Karen, she suddenly recalled. That was the girl's name.

"Your daughter is a dead ringer for you, Dennis," she said, recognizing a man she'd gone to school with from kindergarten through high school. "How are you doing?"

"Good to see you, Jenn. Have you found my wife yet? She's supposed to be working one of these booths, but I can't find her."

"Lori just went over to the rummage sale in the barn," Jenna said. She'd had a few brief minutes to catch up with Lori as they passed each other. She hadn't made the connection with Karen then, but with Dennis it was unmistakable.

"Wonderful. More junk."

"Oh, you're no fun, Dennis," Jenna teased. "I'm sure she'll find something nice to bring home."

"Yeah, Daddy," Karen said, still holding both cotton candy cones in her hands.

"Hey, I thought we were going to *share* a cotton candy, Karen," he said to the little girl with mock disapproval when he saw the two cones.

Karen giggled again. "We are. We're sharing two."

Dennis rolled his eyes at his daughter and then handed Jenna two dollars, which she put in the money drawer.

"We'd better eat these quick if you're going to get washed up for the baseball game," he said.

Karen nodded. "I will."

Turning to Jenna, Dennis said, "See you at the field, Jenn."

With the mention of the baseball game, Jenna's stomach dropped. She hoped Brian's spirits didn't plummet during the game. She'd talked to the pastor about having Brian keep score with Ben, just to give him something to do. Of course, he was happy to give the two of them the honors. But if Brian's heart wasn't in it, it was going to be hard to get through the afternoon.

She sighed. She really wished Tom had agreed to come. At least then Brian would have a diversion worthy enough to keep him satisfied while the other kids played.

It was going to be a long afternoon.

Tag hoisted the last bag of fertilizer into the wheelbarrow and pushed it to the storage shed, dropping it down on the pile he'd already started. The fields were still a mess, only half seeded, but they were coming along. His crops would be late, but he'd made some progress. Whether he'd see any results of his hard work in the form of a good harvest was anyone's guess. But the work was good and kept his mind occupied. And he could always reap the benefits of this work next spring as long as he tended his fields.

Grabbing the handles of the now empty wheelbarrow, he pushed it to the other side of the barn and propped it up against the wall.

His stomach grumbled, letting him know he'd worked longer than his breakfast could hold him. He contemplated going into the house for something to eat, but the thought of spending the time to make something more than just a peanut butter and jelly sandwich, and then sitting down at the table alone, made his stomach protest louder.

Last night he'd fallen into a hole he hadn't been stuck in for a long while. Lately, he'd been more likely to run from the past than to wallow in it. But the guilt that had accompanied his flashback had surged through him until it had nearly choked him. He'd known that opening that box of pictures and letting in those painful regrets would lay him low. What he hadn't expected was for a friend to come along to help pull him back up. He'd still felt troubled after talking to her, but still…cleaner somehow. The fact that she hadn't blamed him made him wonder if he'd been wrong to blame himself and God.

On the walk from the barn to the house, the sunlight hit his face. Even after a year of being free from that prison, he still relished the feel of the sun on his skin after going months holed up in a damp cell.

Lord, there'd been a time I turned to You in my darkest hours.

The silent prayer startled him as well as pained him before he had a chance to finish. He'd left

God behind a long time ago, no longer able to feel comfort there. But Jenna's words from the previous night had him wanting to seek the comfort of his relationship with the Lord again.

Thoughts whirled in his mind. He needed to say them out loud, hear them in his own voice, but each time he tried to voice his feelings, anger shot through him and tears came tumbling out.

"Why did you take them from me?" he asked, looking up at the sky.

Tag knew there'd be no answer in the form of a reply. God usually slapped him upside the head when He was looking to get him to listen, but never in the form of words. Still, he waited for an answer, searching the spattering of clouds mixed in with blue. There was no rhyme or reason in his mind to help him understand why God had to take his family, his precious child, Crystal.

Sighing, he turned toward the barn again, needing more work to help him keep his mind off what he couldn't change. To keep the pain from stabbing his heart every time he remembered how he'd failed his family so miserably.

Jenna had been angry with him for brushing Brian's invitation to the church festival off today. She'd said Brian needed a diversion during the baseball game. Looking back at the sky he'd just yelled at, he realized God couldn't have graced them with a better day for a game. A boy should be able to get out and play, and it was too bad Brian wouldn't be able to enjoy that game with the rest of the kids.

Tag reached for the wheelbarrow and remembered he'd left it in the barn. He might be physically there, but his head sure wasn't.

It was best that he stayed home. Playing baseball or hanging out at some festival wasn't going to get the rest of his fields seeded. He didn't decide to come to Nebraska for the people or parties. He wanted solitude. The festival was the last thing he needed.

Pushing it all away, he grabbed a bag of seed and hoisted it over his shoulder before heading to the barn to get the spreader. He had work to do.

The hot dog she'd eaten too quickly between her shifts was turning over in her stomach now. Jenna finished the last of her soda and dropped the can in the recycle bin by the food stand. Her fingers were still sticky from working with the cotton-candy machine, and she had mustard under her fingernails. She wished she'd thought to bring some moist towelettes to wash her hands a little before heading to the baseball field on the far side of the park.

She passed the Ferris wheel and heard some teenagers screaming as the cars rocked back and forth. She couldn't help but smile. She recalled hearing her father's laughing voice mingle with Brian's squeals of delight as they rode the Ferris wheel together earlier that afternoon. She'd worried Brian wouldn't be tall enough to ride, but he'd stood a hair above the line and his smile had been bigger than the sun when he ran down the roped path toward the amusement ride.

Although her dad wasn't too fond of heights, he'd agreed to join his grandson in the car for the first run. Jenna was glad for any time Brian enjoyed himself. She just hoped his good mood lasted while he sat on the sidelines and watched the other kids play baseball.

"Hey, you two!" she called out when she saw her father and Brian walking toward the field.

As they passed a group of women she knew from church, she caught her father's glance and the quick tip of his baseball hat as he smiled at one particular woman. Mrs. Norling had been widowed for more years than Jenna could remember and still wore her wedding band. It would have been a stretch to ignore the twinkle in her father's eye as the two greeted each other, even though they'd known each other for years.

A pang of jealousy for the loss of her mother was instantly replaced with bittersweet joy. Knowing her father as she did, Jenna doubted he'd ever marry again, but if a simple companionship with Mrs. Norling bloomed into something that put a skip in her dad's step, then Jenna would be happy for him. There was no reason for him to spend his life alone.

Her heart nearly dropped to the ground when she caught a glimpse of Brian's drawn face. She tipped his chin up with her fingers. "Hey, what's got you?"

Ben motioned with his eyes toward the field but commented, "He had a little too much of the Bubble Bounce."

"Did not," Brian grumbled.

"Okay, then *I* had a little too much of the Bubble Bounce. I'm all bounced out," said Ben.

She gave Brian a hug, and they all fell into step as they made their way to the open field with all the others heading out for the game.

"We forgot the lawn chairs," Brian said, pointing to the people who were carrying chairs and coolers in their arms.

"You're not going to need a chair if you're going

to help Grandpa keep score this year. You'll need to be standing to change the numbers."

She glanced over at the scoreboard and saw the cluster of large pine trees was casting a shadow in the area where her father and Brian would be standing. Good. Brian would be out of the sun.

"That's stupid," Brian said, breaking into her thoughts. "I don't feel like doing it. Can't we just go home?"

Brian's sneakers were dragging in the dirt path, kicking up a small cloud of dust. Jenna had to slow her pace to keep from getting ahead of him as they walked.

"Now that's no way to be. The team needs us to cheer them on," she said.

"I don't want to," Brian mumbled.

She stifled a sigh, wishing she could think of something to cheer him up. The crowd hovering near the parking lot of the field drew their attention away from Brian's upset. Her heart leapt to her throat when she recognized Tom's truck parked along the side of the field. On the back of the truck was what looked like half a dozen wheelbarrows. Another half dozen were already on the grass.

Brian's eyes popped open wide, a smile the size

of Nebraska springing to his face, when he finally lifted his head and noticed Tom.

"He came!" he screamed. "You said he wasn't coming, but he came."

Brian broke free of her hand and started to run. The joy she'd felt in seeing Tom was replaced by fear as Brian raced across the ground as fast as he could. Jenna started to run after him, only to feel Ben's hand on her arm, keeping her back.

"Let him go," Ben said gently. "He'll slow down when he's tired. He's had plenty to drink."

Jenna hung back and watched as Brian ran toward the parking lot. He stopped running halfway there and walked the rest of the way. He reached the truck just as Tom pulled the last wheelbarrow out and placed it on the ground. Brian launched himself into Tom's arms.

Her son had a smile on his face, and Jenna felt her lips pull into a grin as well. Tom Garrison had a way of doing that to her, and she would take that blessing and enjoy it for however long she had to enjoy it.

Although in her heart Jenna wanted to run to Tom as Brian had done, she held herself back, walking toward them at a steady pace.

"I hope I'm not too late," Tom said with a tentative smile, fixing his blue eyes on Jenna.

Her heart swelled and she returned the smile. "Right on time," she said.

"Are you going to help me and Grandpa keep score, Tom? Can you?" asked Brian.

"I kind of had another idea in mind, Scout."

Brian's face drooped for just a second, and then he shrugged. "That's okay. I can watch you play ball."

Jenna's heart squeezed as Brian tried hard to put on a brave face. She had nothing but pride for this child that God had given her.

"That's the spirit. We need plenty of people on the sidelines for cheering," Jenna said.

Tag smiled. "Oh, there will be plenty of people doing that. But for right now we need to break up into teams." He pointed to Jenna. "You're going to be on my team."

"What?" said Jenna.

"Mom's going to play baseball?" Brian's laughter did nothing to boost her ego and everything to strike fear into her heart.

"I haven't played sports since gym in high school," she said, shaking her head. "I can't even follow the game, really. I'm just a good cheerleader."

"Anyone can participate, even if you don't know

the game very well." He turned to Brian and lifted his chin with his fingers. "Even you, Scout."

Jenna's heart sank. What was Tom doing?

"Brian can help Dad keep score." She lowered her voice and eyed Tom. "Playing baseball is a little too strenuous for him. Especially in this heat."

"Oh, come on, Mom. Please?"

"No, honey. We've been through this. Remember what Dr. Healy said."

Tom took her by the arm and whispered. "He'll be okay."

She cocked her head to one side and glared at Tom. "No, he won't. He tires too easily and becomes dehydrated fast. Just running the bases—"

"Don't worry. The way this game works, he won't have to run the bases at all and he'll still get to play."

She blinked. "You mean, they're not going to be playing baseball?"

Pastor Robbins came over and said, "Nope. This year we're trying something a little bit different. We're going to be playing barrowball." He laughed and slapped Tom on the shoulder.

"Barrowball? What's that?" Ben asked.

"It was Tom's idea," Pastor Robbins said. "Come, Ben. Help sort everyone into groups.

We're going to need more people on the teams since each person needs a buddy."

Jenna turned to Tom. A small smile played at the corners of his lips. His eyes, clear and warm, just looked back at her.

"What's this all about?" she asked as Brian trotted off with her father and the pastor.

"Barrowball," Tom said quietly.

"This church festival has been holding a baseball game for more years than I care to count. How did you talk Pastor Robbins into changing it to barrowball, whatever that is?"

"Simple. With baseball, only so many people can play and the rest can only sit on the sidelines and watch."

"So?"

"I just explained that there were probably other people who, like Brian, would love to participate but can't for various reasons."

Her insides grew warmer than her sun-kissed cheeks.

"You did this for Brian?" she said, her lips quivering.

"I did this for you, Jenna. I'm sorry about what happened last night. I didn't expect things to get out of hand that way."

"They didn't."

His eyes never left hers and told her more than she'd ever expect to get from words.

"I'm just sorry you had to see me like that."

"I'm not."

His gaze locked on hers. "I could tell you were upset."

"Yes, I was. But mostly for you and what you were going through."

He nodded and was quiet for a second. "Well, I still shouldn't have put that on you."

"I thought we were friends. Isn't that what friends do?"

"Is that what you really want, Jenna? To just be friends? Because I'm not going to lie. I'd like there to be more."

For a brief moment she forgot all the people milling about around them, getting ready for the game, and just focused on Tom.

She opened her mouth to speak, to tell him that their lives were complicated, that she didn't know what the future was going to hold with Brian. As the words reached her lips, she felt something—or rather, someone—collide with her leg.

"Mom! Come on. We need to get on a team."

Brian had her by the arm and was pulling her to the field.

"I guess we'd better go find our spot on the team," she said.

"I guess so," Tom agreed.

Now wasn't really the time for declarations. So she left unsaid the words she wanted to say to answer Tom's question. Did she want her relationship with Tom to just be a companionship? No. But without knowing what their future held, Jenna knew it wasn't fair to pursue more from him than he was able to give.

Chapter Twelve

 ❧

"Come on, Tom. You're playing, too, aren't you? I want you to be on my team!" Brian called out as he ran over. His breathing was labored.

"Look how worn-out he is already. This may not be a good idea, after all," Jenna said, rumpling her son's sweaty locks of hair.

"It'll be fun. And everyone can play. Even you." Tom laughed and grabbed one of the wheelbarrows. "Brian won't do any running, and he can sit in the shade when he's not on the field. We'll go after him to make sure he doesn't stay on base too long. He doesn't have to play the whole game."

"Okay," she said reluctantly. Brian would have the time of his life even if all he could do was go around the bases once. She could give him that much and then make sure he stayed hydrated and out of the sun.

"Everyone, listen," Tom said, wheeling the last wheelbarrow toward the crowd of people. "Here's how the game works. Everyone has a buddy. One person will stand at bat and try to hit the ball. Once you hit the ball, you jump in the wheelbarrow and your partner wheels you around the bases. Whoever bats gets in the wheelbarrow, so figure out who's doing the batting and who's doing the running. All the other rules are the same as regular baseball. We'll rotate wheelbarrows since we need only four. One for each base and one for the batting team at home base. We have extras to keep things moving along. Take a moment and buddy up with someone, and we'll break into teams."

"Tom, can you be my buddy?" Brian asked eagerly.

"Nope, your grandpa is going to be your buddy, Scout."

Ben snorted. "I don't think these legs will move fast enough on their own, let alone while pushing a wheelbarrow with Brian in it. I haven't run bases in years."

"Neither have I, but it'll be good to show these young whippersnappers what we old folk can do," Pastor Robbins said, laughing. "I think I have some wind in me."

"How can I refuse now? I'm up for it if you are, son," Ben said to Brian.

"Yeah!" Brian yelled.

Emotion Jenna had told herself she would not allow to come to the surface rose up and lodged in her throat. Of course, when she'd made that promise to herself, she'd assumed it would be because Brian was disappointed. She had never dreamed today would turn into a day that would bring wonderful memories for her son.

Lord, thank You for bringing this man into our world. I don't know what is in store for us or how I truly feel, but I'll take the gift of today that You've given all of us with thanks.

Tag came back out of the crowd and took Jenna by the hand.

"What are you doing?" she asked.

His grin was lopsided and mischievous. "You're my buddy."

"Your what?"

She was still reeling with disbelief as he dragged her to the sidelines where the rest of the team was already assembled.

Pulling her hand free from his grip, she looked up at him in disbelief. "I can't play."

"Why not?" he said, propping his hands on his hips.

"Because…"

Tom lifted an eyebrow in challenge.

"Don't look at me that way," she told him.

His smile showed a row of straight white teeth. The creases around his eyes were a welcome sight after seeing how devastated he'd been last night. Whatever demons he'd wrestled with, he'd fought and won. Prayers had been answered at least for today.

"You're making fun of me," she said, cocking her head to one side.

"You make it easy."

With a sigh, she rolled her eyes. "I'm glad you're having fun at my expense."

"Brian'll get a kick out of seeing you play, too. Not just shouting from the sidelines. Come on. It'll be fun."

"I don't know."

"I haven't steered you wrong so far, have I?"

She tossed him a crooked smile. "No, you haven't."

"Then trust me."

"So, Coach," Ben said to Tom, "I think we got enough players and we've split into what seems like a fair mix. Who's pitching?"

Dennis, little Karen's dad, stepped up, with her by his side. "I've got a good arm."

"Great," Tom said.

The ball was tossed in Dennis's direction, and they all got in line for their turn at bat.

Jenna eyed Brian with delight. He was positively beaming with joy. Then she turned to Tom who was standing next to her.

"What changed your mind?" she asked quietly enough that Brian wouldn't hear.

Tom was quiet a moment. "I don't know. I guess I just felt like it was time to get out in the land of the living again."

She smiled at that. "I'm glad you did."

After a few people had gone to bat, it was Brian and Ben's turn. Brian stood at the plate and listened as his grandfather told him how to hold the bat.

"Keep your feet slightly parted and your arms high and to your right side," Ben instructed. "Don't let the bat sag behind you, or you won't hit the ball out into the field. It'll end up dropping to the ground. And keep your eye on the ball so you know when to hit it."

"Like this, Grandpa?"

"You've got it, son. And when you hit the ball, don't throw the bat, or you'll give me a black eye."

That got a giggle out of Brian.

"I won't."

The kids from Brian's school were cheering him on, to Brian's delight. The first throw was a strike.

"You're just getting warmed up, Brian," Tom said. "Keep your eye on the ball."

Another pitch was thrown, and this time Brian hit a grounder that slid past the pitcher and went right out to left field.

"Get in, Brian," Ben said.

Brian climbed into the wheelbarrow and Ben took off for first base. Brian bounced around, giggling as the front wheel hit a slight depression in the diamond.

Jenna cupped her hands to her mouth. "Hold on, Brian!"

Tom was laughing. "Did you even know your father could run that fast?"

Jenna laughed, too. "I don't think even he knew he could run that fast."

"Okay, our turn."

Jenna stepped up to home plate. "I hope I can hit this thing. I don't want to humiliate you."

"Why would you do that?"

"I guess I forgot to tell you that I'm totally non-athletic. I'm such a weakling that back in high school I couldn't even do a chin-up in gym."

"Lucky for you, all you need to do is swing the bat. Just remember what your father said. I don't want a black eye, either."

The pitcher threw the ball. Jenna watched as it came toward her, her heart pounding with anticipation and excitement. She'd spent the morning worrying about Brian and whether he was going to have a good time, and she realized to her surprise that she was having a blast herself.

As the ball came closer, she clenched her teeth tight over her bottom lip and swung hard. To her utter amazement, she heard the crack of the ball against the bat and felt the sting of the hit through her arms.

"Get in!" Tom yelled.

Jenna dropped the bat on the ground. She didn't have time to see where the ball was going or judge if she'd even taken a good swing. She just did what she was told and climbed in the wheelbarrow.

Once in it, she crossed her legs and gripped the sides of the wheelbarrow, leaning her body back so she wouldn't bounce out as the front wheel rolled over the ground. She could hear the kids from Brian's class urging him on and some of the people they knew cheering. When they reached first base, she was surprised when Tom didn't stop.

"They're still chasing your ball, and your dad is trying to make it to third," he said, only slightly winded.

She was breathless from laughing. They had just barely hit second base when the ball was returned to the pitcher.

"How are you doing in there?" Tom asked, catching his breath.

"Better than you."

He shrugged. "I'm just fine. You had quite a hit there."

The next batter got into position. He had a serious face, as if he meant serious business. The first two throws were balls. The last throw was the one that he sent soaring into the air.

"That has to be a home run," Tom said.

Not waiting to find out the call, Tom started running. As they turned at third base, Jenna saw her father and Brian glide over home plate. They were right behind.

The crowd was going wild and cheering them on. Jenna could barely hold on to the sides of the wheelbarrow as Tom pushed forward. She leaned back, felt his movement behind her and then closed her eyes.

The crowd, which was jumping up and down,

parted as they made it past home plate. Tom slowed his stride, but his foot must have caught on the base, because he stumbled, tipping the wheelbarrow slightly and causing Jenna to tumble to the ground and roll. Tom flew over her and regained his footing. Ditching the wheelbarrow, he turned quickly to her, his face a mixture of pride and worry.

People were still cheering as the final batting pair whizzed past them as they made it home.

"Are you okay?" Tom said, dropping to the ground next to her.

Jenna couldn't find the words. Her heart exploded with a thousand different emotions. She couldn't remember ever having this much fun. Hearing her father and Brian laughing triumphantly at their good effort for the team only made it more special. Jenna threw back her head as laughter enveloped her from her toes to her head. Tom joined in with her as he realized she was fine. When she could finally get control of herself, she realized tears of laughter were streaming down her face.

When the dust from the play finally settled, Tom reached over and wiped the wetness and dirt off her cheeks. Then he laughed again. "I think I made it worse."

"That's okay. It's nothing a wet rag and a bar of soap can't handle."

"That was a nice play for a weakling."

If she lived a thousand years, she'd never forget his eyes as he looked at her. It seemed as though he were looking through her to her very core.

"You did all the work."

"I didn't hit the ball. You did. All I did was run."

"Oh, yeah. That's all. That's why you're out of breath and I'm not."

"Did you see me, Mommy?" Brian said, jumping into her arms.

"Yes, I did."

"We got a run," Brian declared. "I haven't seen Grandpa run that fast since I turned the tractor on by accident and it started to go into the field all by itself."

"What?" said Tom.

Ben cleared his throat. "That's a story for another time," he said. "Let's hope we never have a repeat of that. I don't think my heart or my legs could handle it."

A repeat of today would be a gift, Jenna thought as Tom helped her to her feet. She had a little boy who had laughed and played like he'd never laughed and played his whole life. And she was laughing uncontrollably with the man who'd managed to make that happen. How could she ask the Lord for anything more?

Chapter Thirteen

They drove back to the farm in Tom's truck in quiet contentment. Jenna tried to remember the last time she'd felt so good and so safe.

Brian was falling asleep against her as they rolled down the driveway toward the farmhouse. Her father was driving behind them. There hadn't been any need for Tom to drive them home since they had their own truck in the festival parking lot. But his offer of a ride and Brian's quick acceptance had made it a done deal.

When they came to a stop, she gently shook Brian to rouse him. "We're home, bud."

Brian lifted his head and waited for Jenna to pull his seat belt off. Her father climbed out of his truck and walked over to help Brian out.

"I'll take him in," Ben said.

"Can't I go play with the piglets?" Brian asked.

Her father replied quickly, "No, the piglets are just fine where they are. In their pen. And that's where they're going to stay, at least until tomorrow."

"But, Grandpa, they're lonely outside."

"Never you mind. They have each other for company," said Ben.

Ben and Brian were still arguing as they walked toward the house.

In the quiet of the truck Jenna found it hard to form the words she wanted to say.

"Thank you for today," she finally managed.

Tom shrugged. "It was the least I could do after yesterday."

"I understand how you feel now. I hope it wasn't too difficult for you."

"Not at all. Did it seem like it?"

"No," she said, smiling. "But what you did today… This was above and beyond. Brian—"

"It was wrong of me to run away from you the way I did. To snap like that at Brian. He's a wonderful kid. I just wish I hadn't upset him."

"You saw him today. He didn't give it a second thought."

"Kids are pretty forgiving. What about you?"

"There's nothing to forgive."

He draped his arm across the back of the seat.

"We can argue about that later. It was never my intention to hurt you, Jenna."

"I know. I don't want you to give last night another thought. You've been hurt enough."

"Not so much that I'm willing to let it hurt you in any way."

She looked at him and placed her hand delicately on his cheek. He might have shaved before he'd come to the field, but stubble was already making his face rough beneath her fingertips.

"I'm not Nancy, any more than you're Kent. Neither one of us can replace what we've lost. And we can't go back and change things."

"No one can. And I'm not asking you to be anything more than who you are."

"That's good to hear. It's hard enough making my own decisions and mistakes." Her chuckle was bittersweet, and she shook her head. "Answer me something. Do you ever wish you'd taken that job at Fort McCoy?"

"I've thought about it," he answered honestly. "I came here to be alone and find some answers, try to get my life back on track. I can't see how that job offer is going to do anything more than put me back where I was. And there's much about where I was that I'm ready to leave behind."

She nodded her understanding. He hadn't said

no. Did that mean that eventually the pull of the military would send him away from Chesterfield and her, just like it had for Kent?

"Good night, Tom."

She leaned across the cab of the truck and kissed him lightly on the lips. He didn't pull away, but he didn't lean into her, either. It was as if that wall he kept so firmly around him was keeping him safe. He'd let it down today, and she liked seeing that side of him. But now the walls were going back up. She was sure the idea that they were starting something they couldn't finish was a risk he didn't want to take. Did she?

As she climbed out of the truck and slammed the door shut, she waved back at Tom. He gave her a wink and shifted the truck into gear.

What surprised her more than anything was how much she didn't want to see him leave. And that was answer enough for her.

Tag navigated the truck around a pothole in the middle of the road and then let the road ahead lead him to his farm. The quiet of the truck seemed so out of place now that Jenna and Brian were no longer there. He didn't like it. It made him see the depths of his loneliness like he hadn't in a long time.

He turned the corner onto his driveway and saw the empty house before him. As usual, the house was dark. Coming home to a cold house was becoming a habit he wasn't so sure he liked anymore.

He never needed a light to show him the way. But Nancy had always remembered to turn the light on so the house was at least inviting when they came home. He never seemed to think of the little things. In fact, he'd flat out forgotten about those things until he noticed Jenna picking up his jacket and hanging it up on the coat rack. Or picking up a dish and washing it before she left.

Little things had a way of feeling so important when they were missed. And he had missed them. He just hadn't realized it until now.

Tag had been dead inside for a long time. Maybe not in body, but in spirit, in emotion. Today he'd felt more alive than he'd felt for quite a while. He'd laughed in a way that made him feel it deep in his chest, in that special place that reminded you that you were alive and life was worth living.

He climbed out of his truck and paused as he reached the top porch step. Turning around, he gazed up at the star-filled sky. "Lord, has it really been that long?" he asked.

The night sky always had a way of making him

feel small, of putting him in his place when he forgot something important. And he had forgotten. He'd forgotten how important love was. That included love for the Lord.

A feeling of warmth wrapped around him, hugging him tight until tears sprang to his eyes. Yeah, he'd walked away from God because of his anger and the pain that had been all too consuming to face. Tag had refused to let Him in and allow His love to heal him. But God had always been there. Just waiting for Tag to be ready to come back, to open his heart again.

"Thank You for today," he said, knowing He would hear him.

Turning back to the dark house, Tag gave a quick laugh. He'd all but abandoned his fields today for a day of fun. But it had been worth it.

The door was unlocked, and he pushed inside into the darkness, running his hand along the wall to flick on the light before closing the door. The sound of the answering machine beeping cut into the quiet. With a quick glance, he saw he had two messages. The first one was from the lumberyard, confirming his delivery of wood, which he planned to use to repair the rotted boards in the barn. The second one was from Wolf.

"Tag, word is you're planning on skipping

D.C. Your CO is still calling the house nonstop, asking about you. Guess he figured since you won't answer your phone, he'd enlist us to help nag. Man, I know how much you always hated ceremony, but this is a big deal. Oma will have a fit if you bail, and I don't want to be here listening to her go off. I'm up, so give me a call whenever you get in. Just so you know, if I don't hear from you, the next call is from Oma."

Tag smiled as he stared at the bright red numbers on the answering machine as it reset itself. Wolf always did know how to press his buttons.

Even if he didn't want to go to D.C. to accept that medal—and it was the last thing he wanted to do right now—Oma would make him. Having survived World War II Germany as a child, dealing with her own father being put in a German prison for not siding with Hitler, their grandmother made no bones about the fact that she was proud of her grandsons for fighting for freedom. He could already picture her sitting right up front during the award ceremony, beaming with pride.

Tag groaned just thinking about it. Sure, he'd never been fond of ceremonies. But this wasn't just about having to drag out his dress whites. He'd stood at attention during plenty of those ceremonies, while some major or general received another stripe or military award. But this ceremony wasn't for them. It was for him. The military wanted to parade him around at the White House like some hero. And Pike's family no doubt would be there to witness it. The thought of it made him sick.

Picking up the phone, Tag figured he'd get the call over with lest he get one of his Oma's tongue-lashings. It'd be good to hear Wolf's voice. He only hoped he didn't have to drudge up the past and bring a bitter ending to what had otherwise been a perfect day.

They'd been gone all day, and what few dishes they'd left in the sink before they'd gone to the festival were now washed, dried and put away. Brian had had the quickest bath he'd ever had, even though there had probably been more dirt on him than on the ground. But he had been wiped out by the day and had immediately fallen asleep with a contented smile on his face.

Jenna walked downstairs and felt the gentle breeze streaming into the house through the screen door. Memories of warm summer evenings invaded her mind. She pushed through the door and stepped onto the porch and found her father leaning against the railing.

"I think you're going to be hard-pressed to get that boy up for Sunday services tomorrow," he said.

Jenna chuckled, holding her hand against her chest. "He's not the only one. And I still have a few hours of work that needs to be done before I can turn in."

Ben brushed his hand over his head and laughed. "I'm pretty tuckered out myself. Hurting in places I forgot I even had, too. It was good to see Brian enjoying himself that way, though."

She couldn't agree more.

"It's a good night," Ben said. "It's a shame to waste it working."

She glanced over at her father, who looked a little uncomfortable. "I have to work, Dad. If I want to get these orders out and get paid, I'll have to put in the time."

She couldn't see her father's face in the dark, but she knew he had something spinning in his mind.

"I don't want you thinking about this farm like it's a burden you have to hold up," he said. "I want you thinking about you and Brian. What's good for you."

"I am. The extra money I make is my contribution to what I want for me and Brian, Dad. Plus, the little extra can go into the savings for later on, when Brian needs a transplant."

"Too much work keeps your mind busy but doesn't exactly leave you much room for anything more than sewing and Brian."

Her heart squeezed.

"Before you go misunderstanding, I'm not thinking about me here. I've gotten along without you girls and your mother for a while now. I love that you and Brian are back. These last months getting to know my grandson have been precious. But that doesn't mean you can't have something for yourself outside of work, family and the farm."

"What are you saying?"

"Tom's a good man, Jenn."

She instinctively glanced toward the driveway, where she'd seen the red taillights of Tom's truck disappear earlier that night. Her eyes still searched, even though she knew he was home.

"I can't argue with that."

Ben sighed and leaned his hands on the railing, looking away from her. "Your mom and I loved nights like this. Perfect for a drive."

Surprised, she said, "I don't ever remember you and Mom going for evening drives."

He shrugged. "Not when you were little. We

couldn't leave you and your sister alone. Being a parent can be hard on the romantic moments in life, but it's not impossible."

She stared wide-eyed at her father, which earned a laugh from him.

"I'm not good at this the way your mother was. She was the one who always knew how to talk to you about boys and such. But she's not here anymore, and so it falls to me."

Her heart tugged with renewed pain. "I still miss her so much."

"Me, too, baby. Me, too. Especially on nights like this, when it seems like the night is calling to me. But there's no sense both of us wasting it."

"I didn't say I was going to waste it," she argued. "I have a lot of sewing to do."

"Girl, what has gotten into you? There was a time I could see the wheels spinning in your and your sister's head about plotting to climb out the window and onto the porch roof just so you could run off and meet boys."

Jenna sputtered, "That was Elaine. Not me."

"But you wanted to. You just weren't as brave as Elaine."

She shrugged. "I was too afraid of getting caught."

"Kent's been gone for a few years now, and you

act like you've forgotten men even exist anymore. And don't tell me you haven't been thinking about Tom Garrison in that way."

Her cheeks flamed. "Dad!"

"I know. I know. I'm not saying this the way I want to."

"Look, we don't have to be having any *boy* talks at my age, Dad. I'm a mother. I know all I need to know about boys."

"But you're a woman, too. That's something your mother would never have let you forget. That much I know."

"Dad," she said quietly, then sighed. She turned the tables on him. "Are you sure you don't want to go see Mrs. Norling for a while?"

He paused, just looking at her for a moment, and then he sighed. "There's nothing going on."

She chuckled softly, ignoring the twinge of jealousy she felt, because she knew it was just that, stupid jealousy. "Dad, you don't have to hide it. I like the woman. I think even Mom would have approved."

"Probably. I don't doubt your mother would be tarring my hide if she knew I'd waited this long to start looking for companionship. But I'm in no rush to change a friendship that has been a long time coming between Virginia and me."

"I don't want us to be holding *you* back, either."

"You could never do that. Besides, neither one of us is in a hurry to make anything different. Virginia and I are good the way we are for right now." He took a step forward. "You're a young woman. There's no reason for you and Tom to turn in at eight o'clock on a Saturday night because we're all dead on our feet."

"It's complicated, Dad. There are things you don't know."

Ben lifted a shoulder. "But you do. That's what's important. I don't need to know the details. I see the way he looks at you. And complicated or not, Tom's a good man. That's important, too."

"Is this your way of giving me your blessing, allowing me to finally sneak out of the house for a secret rendezvous?"

Ben scrubbed his thinning silver hair with his hand. "You didn't ask my permission when you should have, and I don't expect you to ask for it now. But yes, you have my blessing."

"Good, because you couldn't be any more subtle if you kicked me out the door with your boot."

Ben laughed good and hard and looked up at the sky. "This is a good night. It should be enjoyed."

With a deep breath, Jenna turned to her father, tears clinging to her eyes. "Thank you, but..."

He smiled quickly, then nodded. "Go. Brian will be all right."

"I have a lot of work to do," she said and turned away from her father. She didn't know what she was running from more, the conversation or her own desire to climb into that truck and drive over to the Garrison farm.

There was absolutely no way Jenna was going over to Tom's tonight. There were about a billion things that had taken up residence on her to-do list, and she was bent on evicting every single one of them for good.

Fatigue pulled at her as she climbed the stairs to her sewing room. She dragged the chair out in front of her sewing machine and picked up a piece of fabric that she'd already laid the pattern on and cut to size.

Despite the fact that the working light above the sewing machine was on, the moonlight spilled into the small room. She didn't need moonlight or romance. She had a mountain of work to keep her company tonight.

With a defeated sigh, she pulled a bolt of fabric from the pile in the corner and unrolled it. She had work to do.

Chapter Fourteen

The phone call with Wolf hadn't brought him down, as Tag had feared. It was filled with a lot of good memories, mixed with a few that he was able to move past. At least for the moment.

It was clear the family had chosen Wolf to press him about going to the medal ceremony. Tag hadn't committed to going, but he hadn't refused, either. The triumphant sound of Wolf's voice as he hung up made Tag think he'd already lost the battle.

A smile tugged at his lips as he looked out the window. It *had* been a good day. One to help erase a lot of pain and replace it with laughter and new memories. Tomorrow was another day for work and more memories.

He wasn't sure if any day could compare to today.

"I don't know how I ended up here," he said aloud to the night sky. "But I'm glad that I did."

He'd spent many nights screaming at the sky, cursing with a fuming rage at the injustice of what had happened to his family, half expecting to hear the Lord shout back to him. Maybe blame him for being so selfish about choosing the military over Nancy and Crystal. Now he wondered if he'd been screaming too loudly to hear God's answer, or recognize His forgiveness.

Feeling oddly energized despite his busy day, Tag managed nothing more than a few hours of sleep. When he finally woke up and looked out the bedroom window, it was 5:00 a.m. and the morning light was just touching the sky, almost calling to him to get in the air.

He walked downstairs and out onto the porch in his bare feet. The cool, early breeze coming in over the fields bathed his face as the farm—his farm—slowly came into view as dawn lifted.

"I have a feeling this was Your plan all along." He spoke the words quietly as he looked up at the sky, knowing no one but God was going to hear him. But that was okay.

The image of Jenna Atkins's smile flooded his mind. Something that had been dead a long time suddenly burst to life when she was near.

Hearing her laughter at the festival had made Tag think of times before his captivity, when life had been good and he'd felt his world was whole. He'd handled things badly then, made the wrong decisions about what was most important. He'd learned his lesson on that point, and while it had been devastating, he was starting to believe that it had made him stronger. If he had a second chance at happiness, then this time he just might get it right.

Reaching back and securing his hands at the nape of his neck, he watched as the millions of stars that had dotted the blue-black sky just a half hour ago blinked out one by one in the morning light.

He didn't want to be alone for this moment, but it was more than that.

He wanted to be with Jenna.

There was a light on downstairs in the den, which Tag hoped meant someone was awake at the Atkins farm. Jenna had said that she had a lot of sewing to catch up on. Maybe she'd gotten up early to get started before Brian woke up. With any luck, she'd be awake.

Anticipation rolled through him. Within seconds Jenna came bursting out of the front door onto the porch. Despite the porch's shadows, he could see from the light filtering out from the den window that it was her. A smile immediately hit his face, but then he saw the panic in her eyes when she came down the porch steps.

His stomach clenched as the quiet peace he'd been feeling during the drive over shifted into concern. Had something happened? Was that really why she was up so early?

The truck ground to a halt in front of the house. Her bare feet were already crossing the yard as he turned off the engine and climbed out.

"What are you doing here so early?" she called out, watching him as he carefully closed the door without making too much noise. "Is there something wrong?"

Jenna's hair was rumpled, and her eyes showed fatigue, as if she'd been up all night working after the exhausting day they'd had. But there was no fear or worry or distress written there. The troubled lines that normally creased her forehead were gone. It was clear she was glad to see him.

"I hardly slept at all last night. I tried, but I managed only a few hours," he said.

"I slept a few hours, but I've been up since two o'clock. Brian and my father were so tuckered out last night that a bomb could have gone off in the yard and neither of them would have roused."

He stared at her for a few moments, just taking her in completely.

Finally, she said, "Was there something you wanted to tell me?"

"Yes."

Her shoulders slumped—just slightly, but enough for him to know she was bracing herself.

"I wanted to tell you that you're beautiful. I just wanted you to know that."

The smile she gave him transformed her whole face and made it impossible for Tag to breathe. She *was* beautiful, but he wondered how long it had been since she'd heard those words from someone.

"Thank you," she said, touching her cheek with her hand. "Is that really what you came here to say?"

He gave her a crooked grin. "Yeah, pretty much. If you give me a few minutes, I can think of something else, too."

Jenna chuckled as she slowly moved toward him. "Sometimes I forget…" Her expression was a mixture of nervousness and resolve.

"What's that?"

Taking a deep breath, as if she was searching

for courage, she looked away and then back at him again. Even in the darkness, her eyes sought him out and her beauty stole his breath away.

"I'm so many things to so many people. I get pulled in all kinds of directions. Dad needs me to help him out at the farm. My business needs my attention all the time and Brian… Not that I mind. I love my family."

"But?"

"There are so many tasks in a day that need to be done that I forget that there is more to me than just a housekeeper, a business owner, a mother."

"You're a woman," he said.

She nodded.

"I'm not likely to forget that, Jenna. Ever."

"Then remind me."

She launched into his arms. He loved how she seemed to fit so well with him, how her warmth and compassion wrapped around him like a blanket. And the way she filled a void that had long left him empty.

He kissed her sweet lips, lightly at first and then with more meaning, which filled his heart beyond measure.

When he pulled away, he glanced down into her beautiful face. "I see it, Jenna. I see you."

"Do you?"

Tag nodded. Brushing the hair back from her face, he searched her eyes. "How long do you think Brian will sleep?"

"Long enough for you to hold me like this for a while."

"I like having you in my arms, Jenna."

He kissed her again, this time with feeling and determination his words couldn't express.

For a few moments they just held each other as the sky grew brighter with the morning light. Neither one of them spoke. It was as if everything they needed to say had been taken care of and now it was just them, watching the beauty of the morning become the day and enjoying just being with each other.

Contentment was the only word that came to Tag's mind. When was the last time he'd felt as good as he had these last twenty-four hours? He couldn't remember.

"Want to watch the sunrise with me?" he finally asked.

Jenna chuckled. "I thought that's what we were doing."

Her face was pressed against his chest as she looked across the field toward the brightening sky. He felt her words and her laughter reverberate through him.

"I don't mean like this. I mean from the air."

Pulling back, she glanced up at him. The sky had grown bright enough for him to finally see the excitement in her eyes. "Really?"

"Let's go."

Tom held her hand as Jenna ran behind him toward the landing strip. The morning chill made her shudder, something she hadn't felt when she'd been in Tom's arms. The fields looked as if there were a carpet of crystals spread out upon them, created by the morning dew.

She giggled as she ran. Was this a dream? *Lord, even in my wildest dreams I never expected this.* It wasn't a dream, her mind concluded. She wasn't home in her room. She was on Tom's farm and they were about to chase the sunrise, one of God's greatest creations.

They reached the plane, and he opened the door for her, helping her in as he always did. After securing the door, he performed his flight check. Even in his excitement, he didn't rush. But Jenna saw the contentment filling his eyes as he glanced at her. She'd never seen him this way before. But she knew the feeling and felt it deep in her heart as well. And she'd chase it from one end of the sky to the next if it meant being with Tom.

* * *

Jenna avoided her father's face as she walked through the door midmorning, even though she knew she hadn't done a thing to be ashamed of or to confess to. She was a grown woman, and her father had all but booted her out of the house last night while they were on the porch. It just had taken her a bit longer to realize he'd been right.

"Did you get chocolate milk, Mom?" Brian said, bustling up beside her.

She gave him a quick squeeze. "What, sweetie?"

"Grandpa said you'd probably gone to the store. I thought maybe while you were there you might want to get some chocolate milk."

Brian's smile was heartbreaking. Not only because she hadn't come back with the goody he seemed to be waiting for, but because of the reason she'd returned later than she'd expected in the first place. Brian would have loved to watch the sunrise from the plane. Jenna couldn't ever remember seeing anything so beautiful in her life. But if her relationship with Tom really was going where it seemed to be, then maybe there'd be other chances.

She saw the grin that seemed to be pulling at her father's cheeks and realized that he was trying his best to hold back. *What a turnaround from her younger days,* she thought as she pulled the half-filled coffeepot from the coffeemaker and poured herself a cup.

"Ah, no, I didn't get a chance to go to the store, after all."

Lying was something she'd promised herself she'd never do with Brian, but that didn't mean he needed a full explanation. She'd just leave it at that.

"Why don't you get dressed and then help your grandfather with these dishes?" she added. "I need to take a quick shower before we can go to church."

"Is Tom coming, Mom?" Clearly, yesterday had been enough to wipe away the friction between them.

"I don't think so, honey. He's got a lot of work to catch up on."

That was enough to satisfy Brian, to her relief. As she listened to Brian's heavy feet on the stair treads as he bound upstairs, she gave her father a look.

"Chocolate milk?" she said.

"He came up with that on his own. I just suggested that you could have gone to the store."

"Tom stopped by around five, and we watched the sun rise. That's all."

"I wasn't asking for an explanation. I know you've got a good head on your shoulders and you're a good Christian woman." He gave her a quick squeeze. "Must have been a nice sunrise. You're all flushed."

She laughed. "You're impossible. I need to get ready for church."

As she climbed the stairs, she realized things had changed. The whole feel of her life seemed to have shifted this morning as she sat next to Tom in the plane, watching the sun peek its glow over the horizon. He was a man who could make her happy. She was sure of it now—just as she was certain that she could do the same for him. But there still was the nagging doubt. Could she count on him to stay?

What started this morning could very well mean their lives would become worlds apart if Tom decided to return to service again.

It had been a long time since Tag had stepped foot inside a church.

He sat in the parking lot of the church and watched the cars come in and park. It had been a long time since he'd gone to church and he was eager to be in the Lord's house again. Resisting the urge to check his watch, he wondered if Jenna and Brian weren't coming today. Jenna had been exhausted after their flight this morning. He'd managed an hour of sleep before getting ready for church, but she had Brian and it was doubtful he'd let her rest.

He could always go inside alone. Sighing, he pushed the truck door open and stepped out into the sunshine. A smile lit his face when he heard Brian's squeal of delight.

"Hi, Tom!" The sound of feet on the ground barreling toward him grew louder until Brian launched himself into Tag's arms.

"Hey, Scout. You're going to wrinkle your church clothes."

"It's already a done deal," Jenna said. "He's been fidgeting for the last half hour. And we're going to be forced to sit in the back of the church—again—because he couldn't keep his hands off the piglets while I was getting ready."

"We'll sit together." The surprised look on her face told Tag she was pleased. "I figured after yesterday people will be talking. There's no sense pretending the rumors are untrue."

She smiled and looped her arm through his. "That sounds nice."

Brian continued to fidget through the service, ignoring Jenna's hushed scolding to sit quiet, but no one seemed to mind. At least, no one seemed outwardly annoyed. When Crystal was a baby, Tag and Nancy had always taken her to church together when he was on leave. She'd make noise and look up at the lights or church beams.

During one particular service, when Crystal was particularly vocal, the pastor stopped the service and commented that the sound of children talking in church was just proof that they were talking to the Lord. Their voices were pure, and their words understood by God.

As the memory became clearer, Tag was struck by how it didn't pain him to remember. Maybe there was hope that one day the good memories he had would come to the surface without the pain they used to bring.

Tag found the service surprisingly inspiring, particularly when the pastor mentioned the verse John 12:46, which echoed what Tag was feeling so well.

I have come as Light into the world, so that everyone who believes in Me will not remain in darkness.

He'd been in darkness for a very long time, long before he'd come back from Afghanistan and discovered his family was gone. It was only by coming here to Chesterfield, by knowing Jenna and, after her example, opening his heart that he returned to the Lord and saw that guiding love.

He made a mental note to seek the pastor out after church to thank him again for changing the game for Brian at the festival, and to tell him how much he'd enjoyed the service.

Coffee and pastry were served in the rectory after the service. He followed Jenna and Brian to the hall with the others.

"This is Brian's favorite part of church, I'm sorry to say," Jenna said to the pastor.

"He's here. That's what counts." Pastor Robbins turned to Tag. "That was quite the idea you had for the wheelbarrow baseball game yesterday. It was a hit. A lot of people who don't normally participate joined in and enjoyed it a lot. We'll have to make it a tradition."

Tag glanced around the room and saw that Brian was out of earshot over at the buffet table, deciding between a piece of chocolate cake and a brownie. "It made Brian happy. He was really disappointed about not being able to play."

"All the kids play," a woman, who introduced herself as Carol, said as she came up to where he was standing with Jenna and the pastor. "If they want to, that is."

"Brian has an unusual condition," Jenna

explained. "His only kidney is really fragile, and too much exercise without proper hydration is really dangerous. The doctor advised us against him playing because we knew he'd overexert himself just being at the festival. We didn't want to tax his body too much."

Carol nodded. "I didn't realize his condition was that serious. I'm a nurse at the clinic two days a week. I haven't had a chance to meet you and Brian until now, but the doctor did mention we have a patient in town with kidney disease and to be on the alert should he come in. Is that Brian?"

"Unfortunately, yes," said Jenna.

"Is he a candidate for a kidney transplant?" Carol asked.

Jenna shook her head. "Not yet. They don't consider his condition urgent enough. Truthfully, I don't want him to get to the point of being so sick that he'd have to be moved higher on the donor list, either."

"I don't blame you," Carol said. "But family members donate kidneys for transplant all the time, making it easier on the recipient."

"If I could, I'd give him one of my kidneys right now so he could play like that all the time," Jenna said.

"Why can't you?" the pastor asked.

"Aside from the fact that Brian would have to be a little older to accept an adult kidney, my blood type and skin type are wrong for transplant. He's going to have to wait for a donor, when the time comes. Until then, it's dialysis in Valentine a few times a week."

The serious look on Carol's face concerned Tag. He knew of Brian's illness, but he didn't understand just how serious it really was.

"It's really too bad we don't have the funds to get a dialysis machine for the clinic," said Carol. "But there is only so much money to go around and so much this small town needs given that we don't have a full-scale medical facility close by. I just hate to think this little guy will need to do dialysis until he can get a transplant. That's a long haul a couple of times every week for both of you."

"How much does a dialysis machine cost?" Pastor Robbins asked.

Carol thought a second. "It depends. Obviously, a new unit would be much more expensive than a used or refurbished one. And they do have home dialysis machines now, but again, they're very expensive. And with a child, a doctor would want to monitor Brian. Refurbished dialysis equipment can easily be several thousand dollars, depending on its age. A newer one would be three or four times that cost. And then you'd need a trained technician. Like I said, the clinic just doesn't have enough money to invest with only one person in the community needing dialysis."

"That leaves us with a lot of travel time and praying for a donor for when the time comes." Jenna sighed.

"Anyone with the same blood type and tissue type can be a donor?" Tag asked.

"Yes, that's right," Carol said. "As I said, a lot of family members will get tested when a family member needs a donor, and then the doctors will wait for the recipient to be old enough to accept the donor organ if he or she is too young. As long as Brian's condition does not worsen as he grows, there's no reason a donor kidney can't be found ahead of time for when the time is right. Why wait if you can plan ahead?"

"Then I'll get tested," Tag said.

Jenna's eyes filled with tears. "Really? You'd do that?"

"Why not? The Lord gave me two kidneys and I really need only one. There's no reason not to share. It'll be easier on everyone if a donor can be found ahead of time instead of waiting until it becomes an emergency. Brian will be stronger and able to handle the surgery better." Tag took in a deep breath. "Crystal's organs were donated, and so were Nancy's. Someone out there is alive because of their gifts."

"We could hold a donor drive at the clinic," Carol said. "My husband and I got tested and are on the bone marrow registry. You know, a lot of people want to help others but just don't know how they can."

"That's a good place to start. I'm willing to get tested as well," the pastor said. "Even if a match doesn't come up for Brian, we can still hold a fundraiser at the same time to raise money for the clinic to buy a dialysis machine. That way Brian can have his treatments here in Chesterfield and you don't have to make that long trip a couple of times a week."

Tears clung to Jenna's eyes. "This is overwhelming."

"It doesn't have to be. If we can make things a little easier, why not give it a try?" Carol said. "I'll get the okay from the clinic, and maybe we can set up something for next weekend. We'll get the word out quickly."

Jenna couldn't believe the generosity of the people around her. She'd grown up in Chesterfield. She knew exactly what kind hearts most of the people in the community had. When she'd first moved back to Chesterfield, she hadn't felt the need to let people know about Brian's condition. She now realized that had been a mistake. For too long, she'd felt the burden of carrying her fears almost entirely alone, and now with the generosity of the community, she was reminded that she really didn't have to.

Tag had been right. She had a hard time asking for help. She'd forgotten that Chesterfield was a community where you didn't need to ask. People just opened their hearts.

He'd just finished printing the last of the flyers on his home computer when Tag heard a knock on his door. His heart swelled immediately. Jenna had said she'd stop by to pick up the flyers so she and Brian could start putting them up after Brian got home from school. "The door's unlocked!" he called out.

"What are the flyers for? Having a garage sale?"

Tag didn't even have to turn. The smile on his face was immediate as he saw his cousin Wolf's face through the screen door.

"I take it Oma wasn't satisfied with our conversation?"

Wolf gave him a grin. "Did you really think she would be?"

"I guess not."

Wolf laughed. "You should have seen her. She all but put me on the plane. You know how determined she can be. And I wasn't about to argue with her."

"Only because you know you would have lost." Tag opened the screen door and welcomed his cousin inside. "It's good to see you, Wolf. I didn't even hear you drive up."

"Then you're getting soft since you left the military. But you're looking good. Better, anyway."

Tag gave a slight shrug. "Getting there."

They exchanged a brief hug before Wolf dropped his overnight bag on the floor and walked into the kitchen. Tag was glad to see that his cousin knew there was no question about whether he was welcome in Tag's home. They were kin, and it didn't matter where they were in the world; it was a bond that assumed unspoken privileges.

"Your parents send their love," Wolf said quietly. "Your dad wanted to come, but your mom said they shouldn't push you. She'll only come if you invite her. But you didn't hear that from me."

Tag's insides ached just thinking about it. His

parents had had to deal with so much over the past few years. Losing their only grandchild and daughter-in-law at a time when they didn't even know if their son was alive or not. Then all the pain had to be relived again when Tag returned to the States and then made the decision to move to Nebraska. His family hadn't wanted to let him go. He couldn't blame them.

"I'll call them."

To Wolf's credit, he left the subject alone.

"Have you eaten?" Tag asked.

"Plane food. Peanuts. Chips. Can of cola. I could use some real food, though. But if we eat, we're going out. I remember what your cooking was like."

Tag laughed. "I've gotten better. I wish you'd have let me know you were coming in. I would have picked you up in Valentine."

"If I'd told you I was coming, you would have done your best to talk me out of it. And don't say you wouldn't."

"Then I'm glad you didn't. It really is good to see you."

Wolf picked up one of the flyers. "Cute kid. Who is he?"

"A kid from town."

Wolf looked at him knowingly. "Just some

kid, huh?" He dropped the flyer on the table and looked at Tag. He knew better.

"So are you going to jump right into grilling me or wait until you have a full belly?"

"I wasn't planning on making this visit all about D.C."

"Good. Because I'd love to show you around."

"But since you brought it up."

"This isn't about Nancy and Crystal," Tag said.

"I know. But it is about what happened in Afghanistan, and your CO has been pretty determined to get me to convince you to go to the award ceremony. In fact, my phone's been ringing off the hook. A lot of people were saved because of what you did back there."

"And Pike. He paid a bigger price than I did. He didn't come home. I don't need reminders of what happened there. Those memories already visit me every night."

"I'm sure they do," Wolf said, his voice full of sympathy. "And I know you must be feeling pretty raw, but there's a lot of people who want to acknowledge what happened there and the people involved. Including Pike."

"I haven't spoken to Pike's family since I came back." Tag sighed. He really didn't want to relive that memory, either. Pike's fiancée hadn't had to say a word, but her thoughts had been loud and clear. Why had the extremists who'd captured them spared Tag and not Pike? How had Tag been able to finally escape alone?

Wolf obviously sensed Tag pulling back. He took the flyer and read it. "So who is this kid, really? Are you dating his mom?"

Tag couldn't exactly say that his relationship with Jenna wasn't moving in that direction. It was. But sharing this little slice of peace that he'd found in Jenna was harder than he'd anticipated.

"Silence," Wolf said, "says it all. Who is she?"

"My neighbor. Her son has a serious medical condition. I fly them to Valentine a few times a week for treatment. She's a really nice woman. You'd like her. And Oma would love her."

Wolf nodded. "I'm happy for you. Is it serious?"

"I just moved here…but yeah, she's pretty special."

Wolf smiled. Guys didn't exactly go on about feelings, and Tag and Wolf never really had. They didn't have to. They just knew. What little he'd said was enough.

"Sometimes time doesn't mean a thing. It didn't take me more than a week to know I wanted to marry Brooke," Wolf said. "Sometimes you just know."

Tag didn't elaborate more. The only woman he'd ever heard his cousin talk about was a girl he'd met and fallen in love with in college. Unfortunately, the marriage never happened, and it took a long time for Wolf to move forward from it.

"Jenna will be here in a little while. She wanted to cook me dinner tonight and then go out to put up these flyers."

"I hope she cooks better than you."

Tag laughed. "Yeah, she does."

Normally he would have waited to introduce family to an important woman in his life. But today felt like the right time, and Tag knew his cousin would fall head over heels for Jenna and her family. He knew he had.

Chapter Fifteen

Jenna was pleased when Tom took it upon himself to invite his cousin Wolf to join them for lunch rather than visit with him alone back at his house. *Progress,* she thought. They'd made a lot of it over the last few weeks.

They enjoyed a simple lunch of hamburgers and fries and laughed a lot as Wolf and Tom relayed stories of their childhood, much to Brian's delight. But after lunch, when Wolf volunteered to help Jenna clean the kitchen, he wasted no time getting to know Jenna and find out just how deep her relationship with Tom really was.

"I didn't just come here for a visit," Wolf said, sitting at the table as he drank a glass of lemonade.

Confused, Jenna asked, "What did you come here for?"

"Two things, really. If you'd ever met my Oma, then you'd know that once she gets something in her head, it's hard to change her mind. They want to give Tom the Medal of Honor for his service in Afghanistan, but he's determined not to go. Oma sent me in part to change his mind."

"He told me a little about the award ceremony," Jenna admitted, picking up the dirty dishes from the table and dropping them into the sink to ready them for the dishwasher.

Wolf's surprised look brought her back to the night Tom had told her about Crystal and Nancy.

"He didn't tell me much, but I read about some of it in the newspaper and he filled in a little more," she added.

"I'm surprised. He usually doesn't talk about it at all."

"That much I figured out."

Cautiously, Wolf asked, "Did he talk about his family?"

A sadness enveloped Jenna. "Yes, he told me about Nancy and Crystal."

Wolf shrugged. "Maybe coming out to Nebraska was a better idea than any of us thought. Tom seems more at ease than I've seen him in years. You're good for him."

She couldn't help but smile. She felt that her relationship with Tom was growing, but to have validation from someone who knew Tom so well felt good.

"Then I guess he probably also told you about the offer at Fort McCoy."

Jenna placed a dirty dish into the dishwasher. "To be a trainer like you? Yes, though he only mentioned it."

Wolf scrubbed his hand over his head. "Seems we had no reason to worry about him coming to Nebraska like he did."

"He's family. Of course you worry."

"He told me he hasn't made up his mind about taking the job at Fort McCoy. Would you go with Tom if he decided to leave here?"

When she looked at Wolf, she realized his direct question was out of concern and not just being nosiness.

"I don't know," she answered honestly. "I'm not sure a move like that is right for me or my family. Besides, Tom hasn't made his decision yet." And *I already did that once*, she thought as she bit her bottom lip.

Was she really going to walk away from everything she'd just found again, like she had when she'd gotten married to Kent? She'd been fighting with herself for days about what she'd do. But in truth, Tom hadn't asked her how she felt about leaving Chesterfield when he talked about the job offer in Wisconsin. Would he even want her to go with him?

She'd only just found her place here again in Chesterfield, and Brian's place, as well. It wasn't about the what-ifs, which were uncertain. It was about the things she was certain about—home and having the support she'd needed for so long.

"It's a good offer for him," Wolf pointed out. "He can still do what he loves but be home, where he can be with his family. I think he needs this."

"Are you afraid I'll put pressure on him to stay in Chesterfield?"

Wolf shook his head. "Tom has always made his own decisions. I love my cousin. He's been hurt by life enough. But I'd be lying if I said I liked the idea of him staying in Nebraska when so much of what's left of his family wants to be part of his life, too. We miss him. But he's his own person, and it's clear you're special to him."

"It makes things complicated." She didn't expect Wolf to understand her fears and concerns.

"He told me about Brian's condition. There are good hospitals in Wisconsin."

"I don't doubt it. But since you know my son is sick, you must understand that my whole support system is here in Chesterfield."

"Tom's is in Wisconsin. At least, it used to be."

She shook her head. "We're getting ahead of things. Tom hasn't asked me to do anything with him other than put up some flyers for the fundraiser."

Wolf smiled. "Fair enough. I didn't mean to pry."

"You're not. You're just proving what I've suspected for a while."

"What's that?"

"That there is a whole world of Tom's that I don't really know anything about, including his family and how much they really mean to him."

"I'm glad he has a friend in you, Jenna. And since you're a good cook, I'll be sure to pass on the word to the family that he's being well fed."

They both laughed.

Jenna had vowed that when she returned to Chesterfield, she'd put her needs and Brian's first. She'd traveled the world with a man who was never there, and over and over again, he had let her down. She couldn't risk that with Tom, but she knew she was already in too deep to go back and change the way she felt about him.

If the fundraiser went well, then Chesterfield would have everything she and Brian needed except for one thing. If Tom took that job in Wisconsin, at Fort McCoy, it wouldn't have Tom Garrison.

Jenna glanced out the kitchen window and saw that Tom and Brian were headed back toward the house. Tom was staying in Chesterfield, at least for right now. But he had no roots in the town. And after meeting Wolf, Jenna knew he had a strong family connection back in Wisconsin. Maybe his need to hide from the world would subside and he'd decide to take that job at Fort McCoy.

And then there was Brian. Oh, Jenna knew Tom adored Brian. But Tom had already lost a child and was still grieving. No one knew how long Brian would be able to remain healthy or if he'd become sick quickly, like his father, and die before anything could be done to save him. How could she expect Tom to ride the roller coaster of worry that she lived?

As the duo barreled through the kitchen door, Jenna pasted a smile on her face and decided now wasn't the time to think about it. She'd just enjoy what she had right now and let the Lord worry about the rest.

* * *

Spring days had a way of making you feel hope, Jenna thought as she sat in the lobby of the clinic. Earlier in the day Chesterfield Medical had been abuzz with activity like she'd never seen before. A table had been set up in the lobby for people to make donations to the dialysis machine fund. The generosity of the townsfolk had her in tears more than she wanted to admit.

Although she hadn't seen some of the people in years, she recognized many of the faces. All of them gave warm well wishes to both her and Brian. She was equally surprised by the number of people who so willingly came out to give blood and test to see if they were a match to one day give Brian a kidney.

She thanked the Lord endlessly during the day that she lived in a place where the hearts of the people she knew were huge.

By midday the stream of people had slowed to a trickle, and they decided to go home and celebrate with hot fudge sundaes. Back at the farmhouse, Jenna pulled out the tub of chocolate ice cream and the whipped topping and set them on the table.

"Do you like nuts on yours?" she asked as Tom reached up to pull some glass bowls out of the cabinet.

He placed them down on the counter and reached over to the tub she'd just opened to scoop out a generous fingerful.

"I like the works," he said and then reached over for another fingerful.

Jenna swatted his hand away and grabbed a spoon from the drawer, being careful to use her fingers that weren't already sticky from melting ice cream.

"Wolf said you weren't going to the award ceremony in Washington, D.C. Is that true?" she said.

His face went from playful to serious in a matter of seconds. "And he asked you to talk to me?"

She shrugged. "He didn't have to. I offered. He told me about Pike and how he was killed while still in prison with you. Wolf wanted me to understand what you've been through."

"We were plotting an escape. Somehow our captors found out about it. I made it out, but when I got to a place where I was covered, I realized Pike wasn't behind me. He'd been right there, and then he was gone."

"What happened?"

"I can only guess, but I think Pike knew he was caught and decided to hang back and give me a chance to get clear. And since the extremists had someone to give their *attention* to, it worked. I escaped. But Pike was killed."

"I'm sorry."

Tom drew in a deep breath. "I don't want to go to this ceremony alone."

"Wolf said your whole family is going to be there. Your grandparents, your parents and Wolf."

He smiled warmly. "Not everyone. Unless, of course, you and Brian decide to come. If I go, I'd like you both to be there."

A lump formed in her throat. "Brian would love that."

"Maybe we can make a quick stop in Wisconsin on the way back. It might be nice to spend a little more time with my family."

"I'd like that."

Tag reached past her and grabbed another fingerful of ice cream. Unlike the last time, she didn't swat his hand away. Instead, she felt happiness and quiet contentment at the way Tom was behaving as if she and Brian were already part of his family.

"This has already gone a little soft," she said.

"It's best that way."

"Brian thinks so, too. But if he wants to have some before it becomes soup, he'd better get in here." She bent over the sink and hollered out the open kitchen window. "Brian!"

"He said he was going out to the barn," Tom said. "Probably playing with the piglets again."

She looked in the direction of the barn but couldn't see him. "Brian! Ice cream's melting!"

She'd managed to place two messy scoops of ice cream into the first bowl when she was startled by Brian's piercing cry. The spoon slipped from her wet fingers and dropped into the bowl with a clank before bouncing out and crashing to the floor, splattering ice cream. She left it there and raced out the screen door with Tom.

"Brian!" he hollered as he ran.

Jenna's heart pounded in her chest as fear consumed her. She'd heard many cries from her son over the years, but nothing like the one she'd just heard.

When they reached the barn, Brian was sprawled out on his back, writhing in pain as he held his arm. Jenna dropped to her knees alongside Tom.

"What did you do?" she asked.

Through his hysterical tears, Brian confessed, "I tried to jump out of the loft like the soldiers do in training, and I missed the hay bale."

"Oh, no," Tom said.

"What is he talking about?" Jenna said.

"It's my fault." Tom bent over and assessed Brian's arm. "It doesn't look broken, but it could be a bad sprain or a fracture."

"Broken?" she asked Tom. Her panic rose up in her throat. Her baby might have a broken bone? "You're not supposed to be doing things like this, Brian. You know that."

"Let's get going." Tom scooped Brian up in his arms and raced to the truck. "Call the clinic on your cell phone. You have it with you, don't you?"

"There's no service at the house, only on the way to town. My purse is inside. I'll grab it and call once we're on the road."

"I'll meet you in the truck."

Brian was inconsolable. Tears rained down his white cheeks and dropped on his dirty shirt. Every move Tag made caused Brian to cry out. Tag didn't want to extend the pain Brian felt any more than he had to, so he moved quickly, propping Brian up with one hand and opening the truck door with the other.

Carefully, he placed Brian in the middle seat and put his seat belt on.

"Where's Mommy!" Brian cried.

Jenna ran out of the house with her purse and a pillow in her hand. She was out of breath as she climbed into the truck next to Brian. Brian's cries increased as his mother drew him near.

"It's starting to swell," she said. "The ice I shoved in the pillow case should help a little."

"Good thinking," said Tag. "Don't worry, Scout. We'll be there soon."

Tag drove in a fog, not realizing what he was doing as he took each corner. It was as if the truck was driving itself.

"Good," Jenna said. "The doctor is already here. His car is in the parking lot."

After parking the truck by the front door, Tag jumped out and eased Brian into his arms so as not to hurt him any further. Jenna ran ahead into the clinic. Carol was already coming through the door with a wheelchair.

All told, from finding Brian on the ground to getting to the clinic, a total of eight minutes had probably elapsed. Yet, to Tag it felt like a lifetime. How had Jenna survived all these years with this worry? How did any parent?

No matter what had happened to him in that prison, this seemed a thousand times worse. He'd lost a child, but he'd never lived with the constant fear of losing one before. That job always seemed to be left to the one left at home.

* * *

It'd been ten minutes since they'd taken Brian to get his arm x-rayed. Her father had met them at the clinic and accompanied Brian while Jenna went to see if Tom was still in the waiting room. His face had gone ashen when he'd seen Brian on the ground, and he'd been quiet the whole way to the clinic. To her surprise, he was still there.

Tom looked up as she approached, his expression filled with worry, and it broke her heart.

"It's my fault, you know," he said.

"What are you talking about? You weren't even with him."

"I'm the one who told him the story about Army Ranger School training, where we had to learn to rappel from a helicopter. I told him we used to jump onto hay bales from really high up to get us used to landing before doing the real thing. He thought it was cool. I should have known he'd try it himself. He never forgets a story. He was just trying to imitate me."

He pushed himself to his feet and paced, much as she had the first night they'd brought Brian to the hospital in Valentine.

"I'm sorry, too," she said quietly.

"What for?"

"I have no right to expect you to take on my worries with Brian, no matter how I feel about you."

"Jenna, what are you talking about?"

"Listen, Tom. You don't have to stay."

His expression changed from worry to hurt. "I don't want to leave you and Brian," he said.

"And I don't want you to have to relive your loss every time Brian is sick. It's not fair to you. I can't promise you there won't be more days like this. In fact, I can pretty much guarantee Brian's condition will get a whole lot worse before it gets better." She hesitated, not wanting to think about the loss she knew Tom was feeling for his own daughter. "If he gets better at all."

"And what? You figure you're sparing me by... letting me off the hook? Telling me to get lost?"

"Please don't take it the wrong way. I don't want to make this any harder than it has to be. You have to know how much I care about you."

"Are you kidding?"

She crossed her arms over her chest. "No. Look, I know you're a wonderful man and you want to be here for me. You've done so much already."

His jaw tightened. "So I'm a wonderful man that you're tossing to the curb."

"Tom, please. Brian's own father couldn't deal with his medical troubles and he had the same illness. It's what killed Kent. I certainly don't expect you to have to carry that burden. And after all you've been through—"

"You think I'm that much of a heel?"

"No. You're not."

"Just *enough* of a heel to leave you and Brian as soon as things get a little shaky."

Her blue eyes widened. "Tom, I wasn't comparing you—"

"Here's a news flash, Jenna. I'm here. And I'm staying. I'm not going anywhere, no matter how bad it gets. I'm here for the long haul."

"What about that job at the base?"

He frowned. "I'll admit the thought of working with the military, training other soldiers, is tempting. I wouldn't have to leave home on missions, but I would still have my hand in something I love. But I've already told my CO that for right now, I'm happy right where I'm at."

"Really? Is that what you really want?"

Tom smiled. "He kept the offer open and told me to let him know if I changed my mind. I won't do that without talking with you first."

She definitely liked the sound of that. Doing

things together in a partnership, instead of all by herself, was a dream she'd had for a very long time.

"I don't want to hold you back from something that is important to you."

"You're important to me, Jenna. That much I know. I've learned that life is good and each day is a celebration, good and bad. I've seen the dark side of living. It's not pretty." Tom motioned to the hallway they'd taken Brian down to have his X-ray. "What you have here is what life is all about. This is the good stuff. Love. Family. A place to belong, with people who make you feel complete. It's real. It's what makes you want to wake up every day and thank the Lord you're alive. And for the first time in a very long time I *can* thank God I am alive. You did that for me."

"But Brian—"

"You don't know what's going to happen to Brian any more than you know what'll happen to you. No one does. That's God's plan. Isn't that what you told me?"

She nodded.

"I've learned a valuable lesson. You can't stop living because you're afraid of losing again. Brian's father was a fool not to see what he had. I was, too. I pushed what was good in my life aside, expecting it to be there for me when I was good and ready. I'm not going to make that same mistake twice."

"Tom," she said, slipping into his arms, "how did I get blessed to find a man like you?"

"I've been angry at God for a long time, thinking He was punishing me by letting me live after my family died. But you know what? I think He had a different plan for me all along. I just didn't see it."

"What was that?"

"All that time I was praying for a second chance to make things right when Nancy and Crystal were already gone, I think He was bringing me to you and Brian."

Tom held her tight. Jenna didn't think she could get close enough to satisfy herself. He was an incredible man, and she was grateful to have him in her life.

Resting his cheek against her forehead, he said, "I want my life to have you and Brian in it for as long as I'm allowed. And God willing, I'd love there to be more."

"You really mean that?" She reached up and placed her hands on his cheeks and stared into his eyes.

"Yes, I do."

The doctor appeared in the doorway. "I...don't want to interrupt, but I'd like to update you on Brian."

They both turned their attention immediately to the doctor.

"How is he?" Jenna asked. "Is it a bad break?"

"It's a fracture. The break didn't go all the way through the bone," the doctor explained.

Jenna heaved a sigh of relief.

"We're going to set him up with a nice blue cast that he can brag about to his friends at school," said the doctor. "He'll be just fine. I'll come back out in a few to give you instructions on how to care for the cast to prevent Brian from damaging it before the bone heals. Just tell him he needs to wait until he's a little older for skydiving."

Tom smiled awkwardly. "Thank you, Doctor."

"Incidentally, Jenna, I know things can be rough with a sick child. I know how hard it must be on all of you," said the doctor. "But I'd much rather see Brian for an injured arm, doing the things kids are supposed to do at his age, than see him for something critical. Don't worry. I'm sure it's not going to be the only broken bone we see over the years."

As the doctor walked away, Tom turned to Jenna, placing his arms around her shoulders. Tears filled her eyes.

"He's going to be fine," he assured her.

"This time. This time it was a fractured bone. But what if next time it's something worse?"

"Then we deal with it. Together. Don't shut me out. I know for a fact I want to be in the thick of whatever is happening with you and Brian."

"Really?"

"Yes, really."

He kissed her on her forehead and rested his lips against her skin for a long moment.

"I want to do it right, Jenna. I want you to marry me. Let me into your family, into your heart, and I promise you I'll do my best to be there for you always."

Her eyes glistened as she looked up at him. "Of course I'll marry you. Nothing would make me happier, because I love you."

Epilogue

The corridor Tag walked down had become familiar over the past year and a half, since he'd come to Nebraska. He had memorized the nurses' faces and names, had gotten used to the smell of disinfectant and sickness…and life. Despite the tragedy that sometimes touched the lives of people who visited the hospital, life was happening all around him.

Tag pushed through the hospital-room door and found his wife sleeping awkwardly against the guardrail of Brian's hospital bed. In his hands he held two cups of coffee. In his pocket were two granola bars and two rolls of quarters. It was going to be a long day, and trips to the hospital vending machine would be frequent after the night they'd spent racing to Valentine when word came in of a donor kidney for Brian.

Somewhere out there this morning were parents grieving the loss of their child. Tag knew all too well what that grief felt like. But in the end their loss was giving Brian life. Crystal had done the same, and in some small way that eased the pain of losing her. He only prayed that the parents of this precious donor, whose gift Brian was about to receive, took some comfort in that as well.

As Tag eased into the chair on the other side of the bed, Brian's eyes flew open. "She fell asleep again," he said quietly.

Tag set the coffee cups down on the table next to the bed and wrapped Brian's small hand in his. "Pregnant women sleep a lot. Bringing a little sister or brother into the world is tiring for a mom."

Jenna was nearly four months pregnant, and it had just begun to show. There wasn't a day that went by that Tag didn't thank God for his blessings. And today there'd be another one when Brian was given a new kidney.

Brian's bottom lip quivered, showing the boy's fear.

"I know you're scared, Scout."

"Mom will get sad if I cry."

"Mom will not get sad if you cry," Jenna said, rousing from her sleep.

Tears sprang to Tag's eyes. "It's okay to be scared, Brian. A wonderful woman once told me that even heroes cry sometimes."

Jenna looked at Tag and smiled at the reference to their conversation the night he'd told her about the family he'd lost.

"I'm not big and brave like you," Brian said.

"The big will come soon enough," Tag said, rumpling Brian's hair.

"That's right. Don't be in such a rush to grow up," Jenna added.

Then Tag reached in his pocket and pulled out the little case he'd grabbed before leaving for the hospital.

Jenna gasped softly when she saw it in his hands. "You found it," she mouthed quietly.

Jenna had insisted Tag keep the medal he'd been given for his service in Afghanistan, but he'd refused to put it on any type of display. When he'd received it, he'd had the urge to send it back. Since then he had worked through his anger and guilt and was now glad he'd kept the Medal of Honor the president had given him. He'd intended to give it to Brian after his kidney operation, but now seemed like a better time.

Opening the case, he handed it to Brian.

"Wow," was all Brian said when Tag showed him the medal. "Is this your hero's medal?"

"Sure is. This is the one the president of the United States gave me when we all went on that trip to Washington, D.C., before your mom and I got married," Tag replied.

"That was a fun trip, huh, honey?" Jenna said.

Brian nodded.

"You shook the president's hand," Jenna added.

"That's right," Tag said. "I want you to have this medal."

Brian's eyes widened. "Why? I'm not a brave hero."

There were a thousand reasons, and yet no words could adequately describe Tag's feelings for his new family. He couldn't put into words the love he had for Jenna and Brian, or his gratitude for the second chance he'd been given with her love and the new child they'd created. So, he put it plainly in a way Brian could understand.

"Scout, you're my hero. With everything you've gone through, I think you're the biggest and bravest person I've ever met."

Peace settled deep within him with Brian's

bright smile. The tears welling in Jenna's eyes said all the rest. The Lord had given them all a second chance and a blessing that would last a lifetime.

* * * * *

Dear Reader,

I'm so pleased that you picked up *Fresh-Start Family* to read. While I've written several Love Inspired Suspense books, this is my first Love Inspired book and I'm thrilled to be a part of this group of fine authors.

People always ask writers how we come up with our story ideas and character names. In *Fresh-Start Family* my inspiration was easy. I took stories from my husband (another Tom) about his days as a marine and used them as inspiration to create the hero, Tom (Tag) Garrison. Jenna is a young mother who is busy with work and an active seven-year-old son, something we can all relate to. But she has the added burden of living in fear of losing her child to a disease that killed her late husband. This story is about second chances, learning to trust in God and in love in the hard times so you can learn to appreciate the good things in life. I hope you enjoy reading it as much as I did writing it.

Please visit me at the Craftie Ladies of Romance Web site and the Craftie Ladies of Suspense Web site, where Love Inspired and Love Inspired Suspense authors post short stories and have free book giveaways.

http://www.ladiesofsuspense.blogspot.com
http://www.craftieladiesofromance.blogspot.com

Many blessings,
Lisa Mondello

QUESTIONS FOR DISCUSSION

1. Jenna lives in fear of her son getting sicker and dying. How does she rely on her faith to cope with that fear?

2. Have you ever had to make choices in your life regarding someone who was ill? How did your faith play into the choices you made?

3. Why was it so important for Jenna to move back to Chesterfield when her son's best chances for medical treatment were in the big city? Would you have made the same choice?

4. It's common for people to want to run away from what hurts them. How does Tag run away from the tragedies of his life? By running away, does he succeed in escaping his past?

5. Tag has suffered a personal and professional tragedy that he's having difficulty accepting. How does his faith in God play a part in this?

6. What are the events that lead to Tag having flashbacks? How does he move on from them?

7. Although Jenna fears that the very thing Tag is grieving over will happen to her, she still seeks Tag out at the church festival. What do you suppose she is hoping for? Does she find it?

8. Tag avoids talking to his family for a few reasons. When his cousin calls, what is his cousin trying to get Tag to do? What is the real reason Tag is so conflicted about doing it?

9. Tag has distanced himself from more than just his family. He's distanced himself from God. Have you ever distanced yourself from your faith in times of crisis? What made you come back?

10. What events lead to Tag coming around and realizing he needs to open his heart to love and faith again?

11. How does Jenna help Tag open his heart and deal with his grief?

12. Brian needs a kidney transplant, but Jenna knows that the only way Brian will receive the transplant he needs is if another child dies. How does Jenna call on her faith to deal with her conflicting emotions regarding this?

13. How important is the theme of second chances to this story? Have you been in a position where you felt all was lost, only to discover you had a second chance?

LARGER-PRINT BOOKS!

GET 2 FREE
LARGER-PRINT NOVELS
PLUS 2 FREE
MYSTERY GIFTS

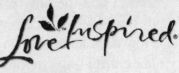

Larger-print novels are now available...

Love Inspired
SUSPENSE
RIVETING INSPIRATIONAL ROMANCE

Watch for our new series of
edge-of-your-seat suspense novels.
These contemporary tales
of intrigue and romance
feature Christian characters
facing challenges to their faith...
and their lives!

NOW AVAILABLE IN REGULAR & LARGER-PRINT FORMATS

Steeple
Hill®

Visit:
www.SteepleHill.com

LISUSDIR10